THE MAKINGS OF A WARRIOR

BOOK FOUR OF THE SYLVAN CHRONICLES

PETER WACHT

The Makings of a Warrior

By Peter Wacht

Book Four of The Sylvan Chronicles

Cover design by Ebooklaunch.com

Published in the United States by Kestrel Media Group LLC.

ISBN: 978-1-950236-06-0

eBook ISBN: 978-1-950236-07-7

Library of Congress Control Number: 2019920372

❀ Created with Vellum

ALSO BY PETER WACHT

THE REALMS OF THE TALENT AND THE CURSE

THE TALES OF CALEDONIA

(Complete 7-Book Series)

Blood on the White Sand (short story)*

The Diamond Thief (short story)*

The Protector

The Protector's Quest

The Protector's Vengeance

The Protector's Sacrifice

The Protector's Reckoning

The Protector's Resolve

The Protector's Victory

TALES OF THE TERRITORIES

A Fate Worse Than Death (short story)*

Stalking the Red Ruby (short story)*

Death on the Burnt Ocean (Forthcoming 2023)

Monsters in the Mist (Forthcoming 2023)

The Dance of the Daggers (Forthcoming 2023)

THE SYLVAN CHRONICLES

(Complete 9-Book Series)

The Legend of the Kestrel

The Call of the Sylvana

The Raptor of the Highlands

The Makings of a Warrior

The Lord of the Highlands

The Lost Kestrel Found

The Claiming of the Highlands

The Fight Against the Dark

The Defender of the Light

THE RISE OF THE SYLVAN WARRIORS

Through the Knife's Edge (short story)*

* Free short stories can be downloaded from my author website at www.PeterWachtBooks.com.

YOUR FREE SHORT STORY IS WAITING

THROUGH THE KNIFE'S EDGE

This short story is a prelude to the events in *The Sylvan Chronicles* and is free to readers who receive my newsletter.

Sign up and get your free copy at www.PeterWachtBooks.com.

1

THE HUNGER

The hunger. It knew only the hunger. A desperate, unrelenting demand, one that could not be denied. As the years passed, the craving to complete its appointed task came and went, yet the hunger remained. To hunt. To kill. Then to hunt once more. It had never failed. It would not have survived for so long if it had. Created for a single purpose, if it failed, it died.

It had been a long time, though, since its last kill. Its hunger had increased as the days, then months, then years passed, becoming almost unbearable. But its prey still eluded it. Until now.

Flexing its arms and shoulders, leathery black wings opened and closed on its back. It had searched for a very long time, but to no avail. Now it could finally satisfy its hunger. Its prey, hidden for so many years, had finally shown itself. It was time to hunt. Time to kill.

2

———————

THE PREY

"Thank you," said Thomas, patting the large black wolf on the back.

Without Beluil's assistance, Thomas very likely would have had his throat torn out by the last Fearhound. Only Beluil's quick action saved him.

Having tracked a pack of Fearhounds around the edge of the Burren, he and Beluil caught up to the beasts as they attacked a patrol from Fal Carrach, which also happened to include Fal Carrach's king, Gregory, and his daughter. Gaining the high ground above the skirmish, Thomas turned the tide with his precise shooting, every arrow striking true to take down a creature. Beluil eliminated the final Fearhound, which had gotten a bit too close for comfort.

Images flashed through Thomas' mind as he and Beluil walked deeper into the eastern part of Burren, slowly making their way back to the Isle of Mist. Harnessing his Talent, Thomas translated the images as "brothers." He understood. They had grown up together, he and Beluil. They were brothers. Other images followed.

"I am not in love," protested Thomas. Beluil relayed more

scenes of the girl Thomas had saved during the struggle with the Fearhounds. "I barely even looked at her."

Thomas' face turned beet red as he disavowed any interest in the raven-haired girl with penetrating blue eyes, much to Beluil's pleasure. The wolf's grin displayed all of his long, sharp teeth. Another image intruded on the others.

"Yes, well, we just won't tell her what happened, will we?"

Thomas eyed the wolf with suspicion. His grandmother Rya, barely five feet tall but with the presence of a queen, knew how to find out things that were supposed to remain secret. If she learned that Thomas and Beluil had taken on an entire pack of Fearhounds so soon after recovering from his injuries, her fury would know no bounds. He knew exactly what she would say, too: "Did we not raise you better, Thomas? You continue to take too many risks. One of these days, one of your decisions will come back to haunt you. And we will not be there to help you."

He understood that Rya just worried about him, and this was how she expressed it, but he really didn't want to sit through another lecture.

"What she doesn't know can't hurt her. Besides—"

A tickle along the back of his neck made him stop, his words forgotten. Beluil halted as well, recognizing the look on Thomas' face. The wolf scanned the forest around them, yet nothing seemed out of place. None of his acute senses warned him of danger. Thomas closed his eyes as the tickle increased in intensity, setting the hair on the back of his neck on end. His eyes would not help him now.

Something stalked them, something deadly. The subtle taint of evil drifted along the edge of his senses, much like a breeze bringing the scent of the sea when you were still a few miles from the coast. Sometimes you could taste the salty tang, sometimes you couldn't. The evil continued to flirt with his senses. It was getting closer, whatever it was, but he couldn't pinpoint its location.

Thomas took hold of the Talent, relishing the power of nature as it flowed within his blood. The trees and bushes around him suddenly buzzed with a new life that was hidden from those unable to harness the natural magic of the world. He extended his senses and searched the surrounding area again. Nothing. Thomas frowned. It had to be there. But where? He tried again, taking in more of the Talent. Yes, there it was. Off to his left. But he still could barely sense it, even though it inched toward him.

Thomas searched his memory as the feeling of evil teased him. Finally he had it. He recognized the source now. He and Beluil could try to escape — the thought of running passed through his mind, and it certainly was enticing — but it would do little good. The evil would continue the hunt until it found its prey; until it found him. The hunter was an assassin, the best the Kingdoms had ever known. At least now Thomas knew what he was up against and could use that to his advantage.

Beluil growled softly. Now he, too, sensed the approaching evil. Thomas reached for more of the Talent. There! He had the creature now. Off to his left for certain, no more than twenty feet away. Thomas relayed the information to Beluil, then opened his eyes and looked to the left with his peripheral vision. Still nothing. It was close to midday now, but the bright sun failed to penetrate the dense canopy of the Burren. The resulting shadows benefited their stalker.

Glad that he still held his sword, Thomas tried to calm his nerves as the evil moved steadily closer. It was a difficult thing to do. Since he couldn't see his enemy he'd have to wait until the creature made its move. That thought frightened him. All of his training urged him to attack. Standing still gave the assassin a potential edge. Now was the time. Strike! Strike now! Thomas managed to rein in his emotions. Patience.

Against this foe, it was the only thing that would allow him to survive.

The seconds passed slowly. Beads of cold sweat formed on his forehead. The evil continued its slow approach, unaware that Thomas tracked its movements. Eighteen feet. Fifteen feet. Thomas' mouth went dry. He resisted the urge to swallow. Soon. Very soon. He looked to his left again with his peripheral vision and this time picked out a shadow darker than the rest. A shadow that moved.

As the evil grew stronger, it felt as if a blacksmith were pounding out a horseshoe inside of Thomas' head. His mind cried out for action. To run or fight. Anything but just stand there. That was suicide. Fight, run, run, fight. Do something! Anything! Thomas ignored the pleas and watched the shadow as it glided toward him. Twelve feet. Ten feet.

Beluil could bear the wait no longer. Finally seeing their attacker clearly, he bared his teeth and leapt into the air, its claws extended. Much to the wolf's surprise, he failed to reach its target. Beluil was frozen in the air, unable to move a muscle. He couldn't even close his jaws to howl in anger. Dark Magic! Thomas made use of his friend's valiant effort, charging forward and swinging his blade with all his might.

Thomas' attack surprised the shadow, as it was not used to any response but fear. It quickly recovered, catching Thomas' sword on an armored forearm and turning it aside.

Just as Thomas had thought — a Nightstalker! That explained the futility of Beluil's attack. He had met one before when traveling with Rynlin. His grandfather had told him never to forget the feeling of evil from that experience, and he hadn't, much to his relief. Otherwise, he would already be dead. Using his Talent, Thomas created a ball of light that hung above his head, illuminating the forest and allowing him to see the assassin clearly.

The Nightstalker towered over Thomas, standing eight feet

tall with its skin the color of black granite. The ball of light hovering in the air prevented the creature from blending into the darkness as was its wont. Shaped like a man, its blood red eyes stared at Thomas. Its hunger was obvious. Thomas understood why his attack had not fazed the Nightstalker. Its body, covered in hard scales, served the same purpose as a soldier's armor.

Before Thomas could make use of the Talent once again, the Nightstalker attacked, swinging its scythe like claws at his face. Thomas parried the blows with his sword, their ferocity sending shivers down his arms. He unsuccessfully tried to break away from the attack. The Nightstalker followed after him, searching for a hole in Thomas' defenses.

Thankfully, the ball of light moved with them, preventing the assassin from slipping back into the shadows. Now out in the open, the Nightstalker pressed forward, its claws coming closer and closer each time to their intended target. If Thomas allowed this to continue, it wouldn't be long before his guts spilled out onto the forest floor.

Catching one of the Nightstalker's claws on his blade, Thomas ducked behind his attacker and ran back toward Beluil, who remained suspended in the air. Finally having some room to operate. Thomas gathered his will. A ball of fire shot from his palm, sizzling through the air toward the Nightstalker. The flames struck the Nightstalker full force, licking all over its body.

But just as quickly as they consumed the assassin, they died out. Thomas' momentary relief turned to worry. That's how Rynlin had killed the other Nightstalker. Why did it fail this time? Nightstalkers often had some skill in Dark Magic, which explained this one's ability to stop Beluil's attack, but he had never expected a Nightstalker to be so powerful.

Thomas had little time to ponder the possible reasons, as the Nightstalker again surged forward in search of blood. The evil grin on its face, exposing its sharp white teeth, almost unnerved Thomas. How was he supposed to defend himself against this creature if neither the sword nor the Talent worked? Thomas met the Nightstalker's attack and allowed the creature to force him backwards. He needed to find a solution. And fast.

As he retreated, parrying the teeth-jarring blows of the Nightstalker, an idea finally came to him. Mastering his will, Thomas drew on the Talent, allowing the power of nature to flow into his sword. He drew more and more of the power until the ancient steel blazed a deep blue.

This time, when the Nightstalker swung its claws toward Thomas' face, the creature danced back in pain. Its dark skin sizzled where it touched the blade. Sensing a shift in the momentum of the duel, Thomas lunged forward, swinging his blade high and low, each time forcing the Nightstalker to defend with an arm or wing. The hunter had become the prey.

The creature's skin burned horribly wherever Thomas' blade touched it. For the first time in its life, the Nightstalker entertained thoughts of escape. The blue flame of the blade blinded the creature, giving Thomas free rein to attack. As the assassin backed away, Thomas followed after relentlessly. Raising his blade above his head, Thomas swung it down with all his might. The Nightstalker moved to defend itself, raising its claws to meet the attack.

The deception worked. In mid-motion, Thomas changed the direction of the blade and brought it in from the side, catching the creature below the shoulder. The pulsating blue blade easily sliced into its skin, digging halfway into its body. The Nightstalker's scream of pain sent chills through Thomas. Tearing the blade out of the creature's body, he jumped back. The Nightstalker fell to its knees, the horrible wound pouring dark red blood onto the forest floor. The look of surprise on the creature's face disintegrated as it collapsed in the grass.

Thomas lowered his blade, a wave of exhaustion rolling over him. He released the Talent and the blue blade winked out, becoming steel once more. Relief spread through him. For the first time in his life he realized just how close he had come to dying. Thomas felt a warm nose on his hand. Beluil stood by his side once more. With the Nightstalker's death, the wolf had gained his freedom from the spell.

"It looks like we're even," said Thomas, patting the wolf affectionately on the head.

3

A VISIT

Killeran sat gloomily in his travel tent, his feet propped up on a footrest. It was all that remained of his fort. Once a symbol of his power in the Highlands, it was now nothing more than a burned out wreck. More than half of his men were dead or deserted, and his center of power, his primary tool for holding sway in the foothills of the Highlands, was destroyed. Even the massive steel cages that once held his Highland slaves were now simply twisted masses of steel.

He took another gulp from his wine bottle, hoping it would help him think. He had to do something quickly. But what? He barely had enough men to protect himself now, even with his warlocks. Some of his surviving reivers who had gone after the escaped Highlanders spoke of the use of Dark Magic. He drained down a quarter of the wine in his bottle. That was absolutely preposterous! No Highlander had displayed such a skill for hundreds of years, much less would have any control over Dark Magic.

Killeran turned his thoughts back to his current dilemma. He had determined that his men had latched on to an excuse, needing some way to explain their incompetence. Killeran didn't care for excuses. He smiled as he remembered the shock on their faces when he ordered them drawn and quartered. He didn't want excuses; he wanted results.

Even worse, he now had no supplies. How was he supposed to rebuild his fort and begin mining again without any wood, or steel, or even more important, workers? Since the destruction of the Black Hole the Highlanders had gone to ground, and he didn't have the ability to pursue them in the higher passes now. As a result, his reivers now had to do the mining themselves. Though they weren't happy about it, the error of their ways had quickly been shown to them by some of the warlocks. However, these two concerns were inconsequential compared to the third. Somehow Rodric had learned of the escape.

Taking another drink from the bottle, he glanced off to the right where he had thrown the crumpled missive from the High King. *I will not tolerate such incompetence,* the bastard had written. *Only a fool would allow two boys to cause such problems. If you cannot handle your affairs properly, then perhaps a new Regent of the Highlands would be in order. And as you know, much like a king or queen, there is only one way to remove a regent from his throne.*

Killeran cursed himself for the thousandth time in the past six weeks. He knew he should have killed those two. He knew it! But he had ignored the warnings that had gone off in his head. And because of it, he huddled in a stinking tent, drinking wine that had almost turned to vinegar and digging out precious little gold and minerals for a High King he despised.

Killeran threw the bottle of wine to the ground in disgust, watching it shatter into a thousand pieces. He wanted to lash out, but at what? He had already punished the few remaining men who had failed to recapture the Highlanders, but the pleasure from that experience had not lasted long enough.

Slouching back in his chair, he ran a hand under his dripping nose. This damn Kingdom! It seemed that this cold had plagued him ever since he entered this cursed wilderness. He had to think. He had to find someone to blame. Otherwise, he would have more to worry about than just a snot-nosed, whiny High King. He'd have to worry about someone who could snuff out his life in—

"Another Nightstalker is dead."

Killeran jumped up from his chair, spinning around. The voice sounded like a hiss, similar to wind escaping through a barely open window. It set Killeran's teeth on edge, yet he could not locate the source. It couldn't be. How could he know so soon? How could he be here?

"I know everything, Killeran. I am everywhere."

Killeran spun around again, looking into the shadows of the tent but finding nothing. His heart raced with terror. How could—

"I am here, Killeran, though you may not see me." The voice was quiet, dangerous, sure of its power. "You do not show me the proper respect."

Killeran immediately dropped to his knees and bowed his head to the ground. "Master, I am sorry." His body shook with terror, and he could do nothing to stop it.

"That's better, Killeran. I'm glad to see that you still retain some of your manners." The raspy voice, though soft, filled the tent with its presence. The power behind the voice terrified him.

"The warlocks failed me, Master," began Killeran, his mind churning at a furious pace in search of an excuse. "If not for them—"

"Save your breath, Killeran. You think to lie to me? To me? I am the Master of Lies, Killeran! Yet you try to trick the Oathbreaker?"

The dry whisper became a shout that shook the tent poles. The structure swayed violently, threatening to collapse.

Killeran sank into the carpet as far as he could, desperate to escape the voice, yet knowing in his heart that he could not. He would never be able to escape. He mumbled something incoherent, his fear usurping his reason.

"You will listen to me, Killeran, and do exactly as I say. Is that understood?"

Killeran nodded his head vigorously, eager to please. Even more eager to stay alive.

"Good. As I said, the Nightstalker is dead. He pursued a green-eyed boy. I'm sure you are familiar with him."

Green-eyed boy? The Kestrel whelp! He had been a fool. A complete fool. Everything came flooding back to him. Months before Chertney had told him to look for a green-eyed boy, but he had not paid much attention. He didn't pay much attention to anything Chertney said. And now look where it had gotten him. But why send a Nightstalker after a boy? And how could the Nightstalker have died? Was that even possible?

"Yes, it's possible," answered the raspy voice, reading Killeran's mind. "I'm glad to see that you admit your incompetence, if only to yourself. I have a new task for you, Killeran. You will succeed this time. If you don't, it will be your last."

Killeran nodded, almost banging his head on the ground. Relief swept through him. Just seconds before he was certain he was about to die. But he had been given a respite, for now. He would make good use of it.

"You will find this boy — this Highlander — and you will eliminate him. Do you understand?"

Killeran nodded.

"He has escaped me for too long."

"Yes, Master. He will be found."

"Good," said the voice. "And to speed you in your task, remember this, Killeran. You have failed me once. Don't fail me again. Otherwise this boy's death will be pleasant compared to your own." Just as quickly as the voice came, it ended.

Killeran remained on his knees, bending his head in

submission for several minutes more. He told himself it was a sign of respect for his Master, and not the result of his paralyzing fear. He was still alive. Killeran sighed with relief and fell forward into the carpet. He would need several more bottles of wine this evening. Several more.

4

ANOTHER SIGHTING

"Rumors of this Raptor continue to grow, milord," said Kael, surveying the activity in front of him.

"What has this Raptor done now?"

Gregory stood next to his Swordmaster as both watched the afternoon's training session. Kael was putting his charges through their paces, having paired them off into dueling pairs. His daughter, Kaylie, was out there as well, matched against Rohn. They were about the same height and both were quick and intelligent, making up for their lack of strength. The skirmish with the Fearhounds convinced Gregory that he should accede to his daughter's demand and allow her to learn how to use a blade.

"A patrol reached a small village at the northwestern edge of the Burren the day before yesterday, drawn by smoke. They found a huge bonfire on the green, and on it burned the bodies of five Ogren."

"And the villagers swear it was the Raptor, correct?"

"Yes, milord, they do."

Gregory smiled and almost wanted to clap, his attention diverted for a moment. Kaylie and Rohn fought to a standstill in the beginning, as each spent several minutes testing the other's defenses. Kaylie had struck the first telling blow with her practice sword, which pleased her father to no end.

Kael had taught them earlier in the day how to sweep the legs out from underneath their opponent. Kaylie used the move to perfection, swinging out with her leg and knocking Rohn to the ground after unbalancing him with several lunges of her blade. Rohn had been so busy defending against the assault that he failed to notice the real attack. Kaylie had won the first round.

Maybe he was a pig-headed fool, Gregory thought. Kaylie had mastered the dagger despite his wanting her to occupy herself in a more lady-like way, and she was well on her way with the sword, though she had only been training for a month. Perhaps he would allow her to take part in the dagger competitions at the upcoming Eastern Festival. If nothing else, it would keep her from pestering him about it, and he could certainly use the respite.

"And did this Raptor happen to have light-brown hair and fierce, green eyes, Kael?"

"I don't know, milord. The Ogren attacked during the night. Before the villagers could mount a defense, the Ogren were dead. They never saw what happened."

Gregory grunted. Just as he had expected. These stories were becoming all too common.

"There is one thing of interest, though, milord. The five Ogren all were killed with arrows through the heart. And it has been reported by several of the villagers that soon after the attack, the howl of a wolf was heard. It may have simply been a coincidence, milord, but who knows."

"Yes, who knows," repeated Gregory.

Wolves rarely visited that part of the forest. Though the evidence was sketchy, his intuition pointed him in one direction. He was certain that the boy who had appeared in the

Burren just a month before and saved him, his daughter, and his soldiers, and the Raptor were one and the same. But he couldn't prove it yet. That brought up an interesting possibility, one added to the puzzle by his daughter. Were the Raptor and the Lost Kestrel one and the same?

Gregory looked across the field, pushing his thoughts aside. Kaylie had once again bested Rohn. Allowing him to advance on her, she had waited for just the right moment to knock his sword out of the way and lunge forward herself, taking him in the gut. Gregory couldn't keep his pride from showing as a huge grin appeared on his face. She was his daughter after all, and perhaps a warrior queen in the making. Maybe she could handle herself in the ring at the Eastern Festival. Who knows? Maybe just as Kaylie hoped she would become the next Alessandra, fabled ruler of the Highland Marchers.

5

____

HOPING TO MEET

"Yes, Beluil, I know she found out what happened the last time we were in the Burren. But we're not going to the Burren this time. Now are you coming with me or not?"

The large black wolf with the patch of white fur across his eyes sat on his haunches, his expression one of recrimination as he watched Thomas. True, they were not going to the Burren. Instead they were going even farther west.

Beluil protested again. The image in Thomas' mind resembled Rya, her chestnut hair strewn about and her eyes burning fire. Though a tiny woman, she resembled a giant when there was cause.

"All she did was yell at us last time. Like I said, we're not going to the Burren, so we shouldn't get into any trouble. We're only going to the Eastern Festival for a few days. We'll be back before they return."

Rynlin and Rya had left the day before to meet Daran at the Breaker. Larger squads of Ogren and packs of Fearhounds had been crossing the Northern Steppes lately, and they wanted to find out why. His grandparents were supposed to be gone for about two weeks. Still, Thomas' reasons for wanting to go to the

Eastern Festival did not seem completely legitimate to Beluil. True, Thomas had never been to a festival before, and Beluil certainly wanted to explore the land west of the Burren, but he didn't think Thomas revealed everything to him.

The image in Thomas' mind changed. In place of Rya stood a girl with raven-black hair and dazzling blue eyes.

"That is not why I want to go to the Eastern Festival," he protested, putting an extra shirt and pair of breeches in his travel sack. He had already collected some dried fruit and cheese. "I told you before. I just want to see what it's like at the festival."

Beluil smirked as he listened to Thomas' sputtering reply. His friend could kid himself all he wanted, but Beluil knew the truth. Oh, well. If Thomas was going to have some fun, he might as well do the same. Rising from his place in front of the fire, Beluil stretched his legs and arched his back, working the stiffness from sleeping curled up like a ball out of his limbs.

"If we happen to bump into her at the Eastern Festival, that's all well and good. But I'm not going to make it a point to find her," said Thomas as they walked out of the cottage and into a cold early morning wind.

Beluil ignored his friend. If Thomas didn't want to admit his attraction to the black-haired girl, that was fine by him. He just hoped he wouldn't have to listen to it the whole way to Tinnakilly.

6

A GAME OF CHESS

Grinding his teeth in frustration, he examined the ceiling of the meeting room, somewhat amused by the frescoes. They showed a triumphant king — Dunmoorian he assumed — receiving a vanquished foe after a bloody battle. The artist certainly had taken considerable license with history. Dunmoor had never conquered anything.

Voices around him regained his attention. This meeting should have ended hours ago, he thought, frowning in irritation. In fact, it should never have even been necessary. His father simply should have told these two what he was going to do, what they would have to do in return, and then be done with it. But these commoners who masqueraded as rulers actually had the gall to defy his father.

Ridiculous. Totally ridiculous. Armagh was the most powerful kingdom on the continent, and his father the most powerful ruler. When he assumed his father's place as High King, these discussions would prove completely unnecessary. He would treat these peasants as nothing more than the vassals they truly were. He would rule, and they would obey.

For the hundredth time Ragin Tessaril, son of the High King, shifted in his high-backed chair. The lack of a cushion on the hard wood was becoming more of an annoyance as the day passed. Yet to sit on a cushion could be perceived as a sign of weakness. That would not do, his father had told him. You can never afford to appear weak. You had to be strong — always.

Perception was all that mattered. The oversized purple robe lined with mink and sable and the heavy gold crown his father wore demonstrated his belief in that theory. His father wanted to remind their guests that Armagh was a sleeping giant, better to be obeyed rather than awakened. Yet, why his father even wanted him here, he didn't know.

For the past three hours Gregory Carlomin of Fal Carrach and Sarelle Makarin of Benewyn had blocked all of his father's plans. Though Loris of Dunmoor sat by his father's side, he was a nonentity in these negotiations. The blank expression on the man's face made you wonder if he had ever had an original thought. It was remarkable, really, that Dunmoor continued to exist as a separate kingdom with such a dolt ruling it.

Many times during the last few hours Ragin wanted to offer his thoughts on the excuses given by Gregory and Sarelle. He stayed quiet, however. His father had been insistent about that. As a result, he had wasted his morning in this musty room watching these two take turns playing the fool.

He should have been out at the Festival with his friends having fun. Sitting in the Tinnakilly palace watching his father fail to achieve any of his goals due to the obstinacy of these two was not what he called a good time. The frustration obvious in his father's voice pulled him back to the conversation once more. Why bother with this charade in the first place? If you were the High King, you should act like it.

"The reports of dark creatures and bandits roaming the borders of the Highlands worry me, Gregory. The time is fast approaching when I will have to take action regarding that Kingdom due to that most despicable of incidents, yet I fear that if I wait much longer there will not be much of the Highlands, or the Highlanders, left."

Rodric looked from Gregory to Sarelle as dispassionately as he could. The past few hours had passed from one failure to the next, as these two repeatedly stymied his desires as innocuously as possible. For most of the items they requested more time to think. With no way for Rodric to force any of the issues, each delay was a victory for them and a defeat for him. That would end soon enough, though. Sooner than they expected, in fact.

"Just what do you propose, Rodric?"

Sarelle glanced to her left before speaking. Seeing the hard glint in Gregory's eyes, she had decided to take the bait. Gregory really was quite handsome with his grey hair and rugged good looks, especially when he was angry, yet she hoped his anger did not get the better of him. Now was not the time.

"Well, as you both know, Lord Killeran of Dunmoor has served as Regent since the death of our beloved brother king, Talyn Kestrel." Rodric bowed his head slightly to acknowledge the man murdered more than five years before.

Of course, Loris barely heard Rodric's words. He spent most of his time glaring at Gregory. There was no love lost between the two adjacent kingdoms, as border skirmishes occurred frequently. Unfortunately, his efforts at intimidation had so far been for naught, as Gregory ignored him.

Loris had considered assassinating Gregory and his daughter while they attended the Eastern Festival. But even he realized that if anything befell the ruling family of Fal Carrach during their stay, the blame would fall squarely on him. Besides, Gregory had brought a large contingent of soldiers with him. Trying to get past his guards was virtually impossible.

The King of Fal Carrach knew his adversary quite well, and Loris' weak chin and scraggly beard did little to enhance the image of strength and imperiousness Loris tried to present. Lately, the Dunmoorian king had talked more and more of challenging Gregory to a duel.

This only confirmed Rodric's suspicion that Loris spent most of his time sitting on his brains. Gregory would kill him in an instant, pleased to remove a thorn from his side. Then again, Rodric mused, maybe he should encourage Loris in this ridiculous idea. The fool was becoming more of a liability as the days passed.

"But Killeran tells me that even he, an able general" — Rodric cursed under his breath, thinking of Killeran's current string of failures — "has had some problems defending the Highlanders from these attacks. Therefore, I propose establishing a small garrison of Armaghian and Dunmoorian soldiers on the southern edge of the Highlands to assist Killeran in his efforts."

Did Rodric think he was a political imbecile? Had his crown finally stopped the flow of oxygen to the man's brain? Gregory could barely stop himself from falling out of his chair and convulsing on the floor in laughter.

Rodric wanted him to allow a garrison of Armaghian soldiers on the Highlands' southern border? On his northern border? Did he really think he would agree to such a request? Such a garrison would function perfectly as a staging point for Rodric to do whatever he wished in the Highlands, or Fal Carrach for that matter. It was totally unacceptable.

For the entire morning Gregory had sat there listening to ridiculous requests — demands, rather — from this pompous bastard who hardly fit into his robe or crown. He'd tell this poppycock just—

Gregory felt a slight nudge in his side. He looked at Sarelle and was rewarded with a glimpse of her dark green eyes. Green eyes that reminded him of a dew-covered forest awakening to the morning's first light. They certainly were beautiful, as was she. Beautiful and clever. But this time her eyes spoke with purpose, warning him to keep his anger in check.

"Your intentions I'm sure are quite honorable," said Gregory. There was a bitter taste to his words. He had no love for diplomacy. Most of the time it involved nothing more than lies and subterfuge, two things he despised. But he understood their value at this particular moment. "Still, I believe this is a subject I must think more on before replying. This is not a decision to be made lightly. From all reports, the Highlanders do not have much to fear from dark creatures, or bandits for that matter. Rather, it seems they must protect against an even more sinister enemy."

Gregory had probably said too much, and Sarelle's sharp elbow to his side confirmed it. Those eyes — dangerous and beautiful. Still, he felt the need to talk more openly so there would be no misunderstanding. He had ruled Fal Carrach since the death of his father, more than twenty years before.

During that time, what he had hated most was having to act like a diplomat. Dancing around an issue was a complete waste of time. He would have preferred a much more direct approach, rather than having to play a game of linguistics and nuances. A game in which Sarelle excelled, and even enjoyed.

"I must agree with Gregory," she said apologetically, as if delaying her decision actually embarrassed her. "The information coming from the Highlands is quite sketchy. For example, this Raptor. No one can confirm whether it is man or beast, or if it truly exists at all. And these thieves and bandits whom others call slavers that are said to be wandering the Highlands. Why is it that Killeran, a supposedly capable commander, has not driven them out? It is most odd, is it not, Gregory?"

The King of Fal Carrach nodded, his expression darker than a moonless night. Both he and Sarelle left little doubt as to whom they thought was responsible for these marauding bands.

"Before we make a decision of such critical import, I believe we must study the matter more," concluded Sarelle.

Rodric's mask of calm almost evaporated. He had talked with these two for most of the morning, getting nowhere. The Eastern Festival had begun as a horse market hundreds of years before, when the nomads living on the Northern Steppes herded their animals down along the border of the Highlands and the Clanwar Desert to sell to the lords, ladies and traders of the Eastern Kingdoms. Over time, the annual event had grown: first expanding to include more trading opportunities, then contests of skill and endurance and other entertainment. Rodric normally looked forward to it, enjoying the pomp and circumstance afforded to someone of his station. Yet this year, the Festival had soured for him, thanks to the two people sitting opposite him.

"As you both wish," acceded Rodric through clenched teeth, thinking of no way to press his point. "We shall wait until we know more, though I truly hope that we do not wait too long for the sake of the Highlanders."

"As Gregory said, your concern is noted," replied Sarelle before Gregory could speak. She had a feeling as to what he might say and did not think it would prove very useful. "Yet, the Highlanders, as I'm sure you well know, are a resourceful people. If they request assistance from either Gregory or myself, I'm sure I can answer for my ruling brother and say that we will of course provide it immediately. But until that request is made, I think speaking further on this topic would not serve much purpose."

Steel covered in silk. That was the perfect way to describe

Sarelle. Gregory sat back in his chair. The implication of what Sarelle had just said was obvious, but she had spoken in such a proper manner, Rodric could not legitimately take offense. Yes, she certainly was clever. He'd have to be more careful around her. He sensed that she'd be able to talk the shirt right off his back without him even knowing it.

"Yes, we will all provide assistance if the Highlanders ask for it," said Rodric, who could barely conceal his rage. His frustration had reached the breaking point. He was the High King, not some snot-nosed flunky to be toyed with. He decided to change the subject.

"That brings me to another matter for discussion, Sarelle. It seems the increasing number of bandits in the Highlands is not isolated to that remote region. In fact, as I'm sure you both know, brigands have become more of a concern for Armagh in the past few months. I've had to increase the number of soldiers assigned to the merchant wagon convoys and ships. Unfortunately, my soldiers can only guard the merchants within my own borders. Once they enter Benewyn or Dunmoor they are open to attack once again. Loris has already given my soldiers permission to accompany Armaghian merchants into Dunmoor, and I was hoping you would do the same for Benewyn. As you well know, trade is the lifeblood of our two kingdoms."

Rodric's request sounded quite reasonable to his own ears. The pleasant, forced smile he wore quickly disappeared.

"I'm sorry, Rodric, but that just won't be possible. My merchants have also told me of the increasing danger they face from brigands, yet they tell me they have nothing to fear until they enter Armagh. Remarkably, some say that almost all of the bands of marauders and thieves are made up of Armaghian farmers and peasants who can no longer pay the taxes levied upon them by you, but that is only a rumor. Until I have conclusive proof that these attacks are occurring within my borders, I must table your request."

And feisty, thought Gregory, as he took in her flashing green eyes once again. His morning may have been wasted, but the last few minutes had been quite entertaining.

7

NEW TARGET

His father's anger was clear to Ragin, though perhaps not to Gregory and Sarelle. Ragin had learned at a very early age that there were certain times to avoid Rodric. Those usually involved his father's face turning dark red with fury or the blood vessel in his forehead threatening to explode.

These "talks," as they were called, were a waste of time. Loris was no help to his father. He only stared at Gregory, his hatred plain. Gregory and Sarelle were of one mind, of course. So his father wasted his time and breath.

Sarelle, now she was quite a beautiful woman, though perhaps a bit too old for his taste. He preferred younger women. Women who knew less of the world than he did, and therefore were more malleable to his whims and desires. A smirk popped onto his face. Yes, he certainly did prefer women he could manipulate. It made things so much easier. Sarelle wasn't quite to his taste, but Gregory's daughter certainly was.

He had met Kaylie several years before, and at the time she wasn't much to look at, at least by his own standards. Though the same age, by then he had already discovered the pleasures offered by women, or taken if the woman proved reluctant.

There were many advantages to being a prince, he acknowledged.

But the passing years had certainly blessed Kaylie. The gangly girl was now remarkably beautiful, with eyes that could steal a man's soul and a body to match. Ragin found her hard to resist. Perhaps even more so because she hadn't yet learned the power she held over men.

His smirk changed to a sneer for an instant. Unlike his dear sister Corelia. She, on the other hand, had learned early on of the charms she could employ against a man, and made frequent use of them. Yes, Kaylie was a virgin in more ways than one, he guessed. And who better to show her the full pleasure of life than himself. Besides, his father was having little luck persuading Gregory and Sarelle to give in on any of the issues of concern to Armagh. Where his father failed, perhaps he could succeed.

Ragin sat up a little straighter, an idea forming. Sometimes a more subtle approach worked better than a direct one. If what he and his father desired could not be obtained through Gregory, perhaps it could be won through an unknowing, yet beautiful, princess. Ragin sat there trying not to laugh at his own brilliance. The remainder of the discussions were of no consequence to him now. He had his own plan to put into motion.

8

BATTLE OF WILLS

"Gregory, I truly must insist as High King!" said Rodric, his teeth clenched in anger.

If he had his way, he would have plunged a dagger into Gregory's heart and be done with it. Trying to get any type of concession out of him was like wringing water from a stone. His repeated failures wore on his already frayed nerves.

Sarelle sat back in her chair, trying to push her way into the woodwork. The discussion had suddenly turned dangerous. Though Rodric shouted at him — something considered extremely bad manners when talking with a fellow ruler, if not a direct insult — Gregory sat there calmly. Too calmly.

One of Sarelle's first lessons as a queen was that most of the time you could read a person's eyes and discern their intentions. As some long-forgotten philosopher had said, the eyes were the windows to a person's soul. Gregory's now resembled an animal's — sharp, focused, offering just a hint of danger right before it was about to strike.

"Gentlemen," said Sarelle, rising from her chair and walking behind it, "I am sorry to interrupt, but I fear I must leave you.

There are other matters I must attend to today. Perhaps we can continue our conversation at a later time?"

"Yes, that is a good idea, Sarelle," said Gregory, his voice a whisper. "There are other things I must do today as well. Please allow me to walk you to your rooms."

"Thank you, Gregory. That would be most kind."

Gregory rose from his chair and walked over to Sarelle, offering her his arm. She gladly took it. They headed for the closed doors. The servant stationed there, surprised to see the two rulers leave, almost fell over himself opening the door.

This was most irregular. No one ever left King Rodric's presence without his express permission. They were almost out into the hallway when Rodric rose from his chair and placed his hands on his hips.

"Gregory, this conversation is not over. I am the High King, and it will end when I say it ends."

"You may continue to talk to your heart's content, Rodric," replied Gregory. "But your attempts at playing High King hold no sway with me." Gregory turned around to face his opponent. Sarelle turned with him, reluctantly letting go of his arm. "I applaud your concern for the Highlands, yet I also understand your desires with respect to that Kingdom. Quite well, in fact. Talyn Kestrel is not here, nor is any other Highlander who can speak for that Kingdom, so that task falls to me."

"You have no right to do such a—"

"I have every right!" shouted Gregory, his anger finally boiling over. Sarelle looked at the man to her left in a new light. A quiet man, certainly, but also passionate. A true king. "If no one else will defend the Highlands, then I will. You know the law as well as I. The appointed time has not yet come, and until it does, you will keep your soldiers out of the Highlands. If I see one Armaghian soldier anywhere in the Eastern Kingdoms — just one — I will take swift action to remedy that situation."

"How dare you threaten me!" shrieked Rodric, stepping off the platform upon which his chair sat. His kingly appearance immediately diminished. Rodric's voice came out in a shrill scream, the vein in his forehead beating furiously. Ragin sat there calmly, jolted from his thoughts. Things were finally getting interesting.

"No, Rodric, I am not threatening you. I'm telling you a fact. You will wait as the law prescribes." Gregory spun and was about to usher Sarelle out of the room, but he turned back around abruptly.

"You know, Rodric, it is rumored that when Talyn Kestrel and his son were murdered, the grandson escaped. Though no evidence was ever found to support that conclusion, there are many who still believe the child lives."

"Rumors, Gregory," said Rodric. Gregory was getting very close to one of Rodric's greatest concerns. If only Killeran had done as he was supposed to! "Only rumors, Gregory."

Sarelle watched the High King intently. She had a knack for picking up certain signals from the way a person talked, or walked, or sat, or held a hand. It was one of the reasons she was such a shrewd negotiator. Rodric's anger had dissipated, replaced by an unexpected nervousness. That pointed to something important. But what?

"Yes, perhaps a rumor. Then again, rumors have an ugly habit of becoming truth. Your Lord Killeran has tried very hard to subdue the Highlanders, but he has failed to break their spirit. If that child still lives, he is of an age to become Lord of the Highlands. If that happens, he will light a fire under the Highlanders that will not be easily dampened."

Rodric stared at Gregory for a moment, his mouth hanging open from shock. How could he have known the truth about Killeran? He closed his mouth abruptly. Maybe he didn't and was just guessing. No matter. Rodric had given it away, and the understanding in Sarelle's eyes confirmed it. Gregory and

Sarelle walked toward the door, the servant holding it for them bowing deeply at the waist.

"Gregory!" shouted Rodric. He was certain he knew the answer, yet he could not keep himself from asking. "If this rumor were true, who would you support? Some Highland whelp or me?"

Gregory turned slowly this time, the gleam in his eye giving him a devilish appearance. He laughed softly. To even ask such a question showed Rodric for a fool.

"Rodric, what I do, I do for Fal Carrach. I have heard other rumors as well regarding the Highlands in recent years, rumors that relate to the terrible night when my friend Talyn Kestrel died. Rumors that sound very much like the truth. If I find out these rumors are the truth, you can be certain that I will act upon them — quickly and decisively. For years, I have waited to assist the Highlanders, but they have not asked, and I can do nothing until then. If I were you, Rodric, I would concern myself more with what will happen when the Highlands stir. They are a vengeful people. If those rumors become reality, I will be the least of your concerns. Beware the Marchers when they come down from their mountain hideaways. They're an unforgiving people."

9

TWO SUITORS

"Yes, Maddan is cute," sighed Kaylie. This was not one of her favorite topics. All her friends enjoyed talking about boys, sometimes explicitly. She felt such things should be kept private. "But I've known him since I was a little girl and he's much too arrogant. And there's a meanness to him that most fail to see. He thinks his father's money can get him anything he desires. I want to meet someone exciting, adventurous, different. Someone who could make my blood boil with anticipation."

The picture of what she wanted, or rather whom, stared back at her in her mind, yet she was unwilling to describe the image to her friends. "Maddan is not that person."

"Maybe not," said Lissa. "But he is rich, and though his money may bother you, it doesn't bother me." The tall blond twisted a curl of her hair in her hand as she thought about it. "Then again, I do like muscle, and Eric has quite a lot of that."

She had flirted with Eric for years while growing up in the Rock, mesmerized by his barrel-like chest and massive arms. Yet, she found the allure of money hard to resist.

"Compared to some of the other men I've seen since I've

been here," said Jenna, a mischievous light in her eyes, "I'd have to agree with Kaylie."

"That only stands to reason," giggled Lissa. "You've had your eye on that soldier from Benewyn for quite a while. What's his name again?"

"Berral," answered Jenna dreamily, savoring the name. "I hope Erinn gets here soon. If she doesn't, we'll have to leave without her."

"You're hopeless, Jenna," said Kaylie with a grin. "Absolutely hopeless."

Jenna had walked around in a daze ever since she met Berral. Kaylie hoped that if she ever fell for someone, she wouldn't appear as love struck as her friend. It just wouldn't be proper.

Kaylie and her friends continued to wander the halls of the Tinnakilly palace. It was almost noon and Erinn had not yet appeared. They all hoped she would soon. Otherwise they'd be late to the Festival, as Jenna had reminded them constantly for the past twenty minutes. Berral was taking part in the archery competition and she didn't want to miss it.

"We'll give her a few more minutes," said Kaylie.

Dark marble shot through with white made up the hallway floor. From the walls centuries-old tapestries, once bright and vibrant, now dull and worn, hung limply. The decoration of the Palace, as the ancient fortress was called, was meant to impress, but all Kaylie got from it was a sense of age and disrepair. Thus the term The Decaying City, used so frequently by merchants and other visitors. To her it was the perfect metaphor for the Kingdom itself and the man who ruled it.

"Maddan might not be to your taste," said Lissa, her pouty mouth scrunched up as she tried to concentrate. "Perhaps someone else then." She smiled wickedly. "Perhaps a certain prince with dark curly hair and a wonderful smile."

"Ragin?" she asked in surprise.

"At your service, Kaylie. What can I do for you?"

Kaylie spun, put off balance by the bright smile of Ragin, Prince of Armagh. He was probably the most handsome man she had ever laid eyes on. His dark curly hair framed his face perfectly, and his smile made her knees wobble with uncertainty. She struggled to regain her composure.

"Nothing, Ragin. Nothing at all. Maddan," she said flatly.

Maddan stood behind Ragin, unwilling to step forward. After their encounter in the training yard, he had kept his distance. Though the same age, Maddan acted like an annoying little brother when around Ragin.

Kaylie adopted the cool tone she had mastered at her father's court, its familiarity giving her confidence. Still, her knees wavered and she couldn't pull her eyes away from that smile.

"Shouldn't you be down at the Festival?"

"Actually, we were on our way there. I thought that you and your friends might like to accompany Maddan, myself and a few of my friends. We are all taking part in the archery competition, and I would hate for you to miss it."

"You really should come, Kaylie," piped in Maddan, stepping out of Ragin's shadow, but not coming too close to her. In all other things he would defer to Ragin, but not with Kaylie. He had set his sights on her several years before — not entirely for the best of reasons — and was unwilling to let go. "I plan to win it this year."

His need to stand out had gotten the better of him, and several of the boys standing behind him snickered at the statement. Maddan was certainly not known for his skill with a bow, or with any other weapon for that matter.

"I think not, Maddan," said Jenna. "I'm quite sure Berral will beat you."

Maddan was about to reply sharply, but a strong hand on his arm held back his words. Ragin spoke instead.

"Berral of Benewyn? Yes, he is very good with a bow. He probably will beat Maddan. But he will not beat me. It will be fun to take him on, Jenna, and defeat him."

"Perhaps we will join you," said Kaylie, seeing Jenna's expression turn dark. In her current state with respect to Berral, Ragin's last comment came close to an insult. "We're just waiting for a friend. Why don't we meet down in the courtyard in ten minutes?"

"As you wish, Kaylie," said Ragin, his smile dark and strangely knowing, yet inviting. "I shall win the competition for you, so don't be late."

The flash of anger that crossed Maddan's face could only be seen by Kaylie, as it had come and gone so quickly. Wonderful. Now she'd have two boys pestering her constantly. Ragin turned to go, but before Kaylie could react, he grabbed her hand and kissed it gently.

"Ten minutes."

Lissa stepped forward as the boys sauntered off down the hall, Maddan the last of the group, his face red with anger.

"As I said, Kaylie, a dark-haired man with a wonderful smile. He's just the one for you, and he obviously likes you." She giggled shrilly. Kaylie found it annoying, though most of the boys Lissa pursued obviously loved it. "Did you see how he held onto your hand after kissing it? All you have to do is reel him in, and that certainly won't be too hard."

Kaylie watched the boys until they disappeared around a corner. "Yes, well, maybe I could. But I'm not sure I want to."

"Not want to?" asked Jenna in shock, her anger over Ragin's statement regarding Berral instantly gone. "Even I have to admit that Ragin is quite a catch. He's handsome. He's charming. Some say he's the best swordsman in all the Kingdoms, despite his youth. And he's a prince! How could you not want to?"

"Well, he is all that," agreed Kaylie, remembering his wonderful smile.

"Then what's the problem?" asked Lissa. She, too, couldn't understand her friend's indecision.

"I don't know," said Kaylie, her expression thoughtful. "I can't put my finger on it, but there's a part of me that says I would be making a huge mistake. He has much to offer, but in some way I can't describe, he is sadly lacking."

"Well, if I were you," said Lissa, "I wouldn't listen to that part."

Kaylie shook her head in frustration. What was it about Ragin that bothered her? No matter. She could think about it later.

"Come on. Let's find Erinn so we can go down to the Festival. These hallways depress me."

10

DAGGERS

"I think Ragin has taken a liking to you," said Erinn, who had finally caught up to her friends. The sandy-haired beauty laughed softly. "This is perfect — the Prince of Armagh in love with the Princess of Fal Carrach. It would be the greatest wedding in the history of the Kingdoms!"

Kaylie threw her friend a withering glare.

"Erinn, I've had quite enough of that," she said testily. "I'd like to enjoy the Festival if you don't mind."

"A lover's quarrel?" asked Lissa coyly. "So soon?"

Kaylie sighed in frustration and walked a few steps in front of her friends. They were absolutely impossible! Thank the stars that Jenna was too infatuated with Berral to know right from left. She had gone ahead of the others, not wanting to risk missing her new love compete. Otherwise Kaylie would never hear the end of it, as Jenna was the worst of the lot. Kaylie tried to close her mind to the whispered conversation and giggling that continued behind her.

Try as she might, though, her anger was wasted on her friends. No, the true cause for her current irritation was Ragin. He had no right, absolutely no right, to do what he did, and in full view of everyone! No right! Kaylie's face reddened at the memory.

She and her friends had met Ragin, Maddan and the other boys at the gate. But since Erinn had not yet arrived, the boys decided to go on while Kaylie, Lissa and Jenna waited. Before going, Ragin had embarrassed Kaylie in a way that she would not soon forgive. Dropping to one knee, he had taken her hand in his own and stared at her with steadfast eyes.

"Come soon, my sweet, for my victory will be nothing without you," he had said.

Completely taken aback, she had stood there like a fool and let him kiss her hand a second time. Her face flushed even more as the memory played through her mind.

Of course, Lissa had loved it, as did Erinn as soon as she heard. Kaylie was certain that by the end of the day, as the gossip spread throughout the Palace, she would be engaged to Ragin with a wedding planned.

She growled in irritation, startling a mother and her two young children who walked beside her. The woman pulled her children over to a booth, a look of fear on her face. Kaylie sighed, sorry for scaring the poor woman. This trip wasn't working out as she had hoped.

The Eastern Festival took place every two years, and Kaylie was finally of an age to enjoy it. The last time she was here her father had barely let her out of his sight. This time, though she had more time to herself, he was still much too overbearing, in her opinion. She loved her father — she truly did — but sometimes his overprotectiveness irritated her to an extreme.

A supervised walk through the Festival was not her idea of fun. Nor was the fact that he had refused to let her take part in the dagger competition held the day before yesterday. Just thinking about it set her anger on a slow burn for the hundredth time in two days.

Not trusting her to heed his wishes, her father had accompanied her to the contest. She had sat there in frustration as she matched her skills against those of the other competitors in her own mind. When the event concluded, she decided that she could have won it easily. She said as much to her father, also pointing out that no one had been killed; just a few broken arms and wrists was all, and she was too quick to let that happen to her. He just smiled and offered a noncommittal, "Perhaps."

That was bad enough, since her father had initially said she could take part then abruptly changed his mind. But having to deal with Ragin threatened to put her in a foul mood for the remainder of her time in Tinnakilly. Well, she wouldn't let one bad moment ruin her day. People could think whatever they want. Ragin was mistaken if he thought his supposedly gallant display had won her over. Handsome he might be, but there was still something about him that bothered her.

Attempting to put her anger aside, she tried to approach the Festival with a new perspective, surveying all the commotion around her as if for the first time. The colors of the booths and banners bombarded her. Nothing, not even the stools the hawkers sat on while plying their wares, matched anything else. Red, green and purple mixed with blue, pink and orange. It was almost too much for her, as the multitude of colors dazzled her senses.

The Festival was located on the edge of Tinnakilly, where the land sloped down from the heights holding the Palace to a long, flat plain. Most of the merchants and traders from the Eastern Kingdoms made it a point to attend the Festival. One good sale to a noble could mean a contract that would keep them in business for a year or more.

She smiled as she took in the scene before her. Off to her left a very large woman sold candy and treats, while the man next to her peddled pots, pans, teakettles and more. They must have been of very good quality, as fully a dozen women crowded around his stall examining his wares. Another man sold vegetables and fruits just a little farther down the street, and right next door some industrious person had set up a large tent offering ale and entertainment. Kaylie almost swallowed her tongue when one of the serving women stepped out from under the tent. Her blouse did little to hide her ample cleavage. That would explain the huge number of patrons at the bar.

Dozens of stalls lined Kaylie's path, but with the crowd pressing around her, trying to visit any one in particular proved difficult. She had just passed the tavern when the next booth caught her eye. A blacksmith's shop, with several beautifully made daggers lining the wood counter. She was about to force her way through the crowd when her friends caught up to her.

"You're not going to be a stick in the mud the whole day, are you, Kaylie?" Lissa gave her friend a sweet smile laced with vinegar. "We're sorry. We really are."

Kaylie looked at her two friends with suspicion. She knew them too well to take Lissa's apology as sincere.

"Really, Kaylie, we promise," said Erinn earnestly. "We won't tease you anymore."

Kaylie waited a moment before answering, then decided that trying to hold onto her anger probably wasn't worth the effort.

"All right, but I don't want to hear about Ragin for the rest of the day."

Both her friends nodded solemnly, though their eyes twinkled with mischief. Kaylie doubted that they would hold to their promise for more than a few minutes.

"You know, Kaylie, if Ragin or Maddan aren't to your taste, perhaps another archer," suggested Lissa.

"Yes, what about that one?" asked Erinn, pointing to a man with a short black beard and long curly hair. He carried a long bow in one hand and a quiver of arrows in the other as he made his way through the crowd toward the archery field at the edge of the Festival grounds.

"You two are impossible," laughed Kaylie. "If all you do is think about boys, how do you have time for anything else?"

"We do not spend all our time thinking about boys," protested Erinn. "There is simply not much else for us to think about except for boys."

"Well, then, if that's the case, don't let me stop you. I'll catch up to you at the archery competition. I want to stop in that shop over there."

"Daggers," said Lissa with thinly veiled contempt, her face screwing up into a look of distaste. "I should have guessed. Come along, Erinn. I have a feeling that our Warrior Princess will be occupied for some time."

11

A SIGHTING

Kaylie watched her two friends vanish into the crowd, secretly pleased to be on her own. She immediately pushed her way to the blacksmith's stall.

The daggers actually were of a better quality than she expected, and judging by the prices the blacksmith knew it. The large man, his corded arms bulging out from a long black leather vest, didn't try to sell her anything, as he sat comfortably in the back of the stall. He didn't have to. The daggers sold themselves.

She fingered three or four, testing their weight and balance, before one caught her eye. She picked it up and marveled at its beauty. The smooth blue steel shined brightly, the sun glancing off the intricate carvings in both sides of the blade. The handle was wrapped tightly in leather dyed blue to match the blade. It was a rather simple design, but as she hefted the blade, it felt as if it were made just for her.

"How much?"

"Two golds," replied the blacksmith. He answered confidently, knowing the worth of his work.

It was a hefty price, but Kaylie didn't bother to haggle. She didn't want to insult him. Handing over her money she turned away from the stand, grinning from ear to ear. She forgot about the dagger in an instant.

A flash of movement across the crowded street caught her eye. A boy about her own age had just exited from under the canopy of a stall, a bow and quiver of arrows strung over one shoulder. Why he would stand out so, she could never guess. But for some reason, her eyes went to him immediately. He looked remarkably familiar. But why?

His light brown hair was short, unlike the boys she knew. The young nobles and merchants currently wore their hair long. Not only out of style, he wasn't even particularly handsome. Still, she stared at him for several seconds before realizing that she was about to lose sight of him. Kaylie quickly pushed the dagger into her belt and jumped into the shifting mass of people.

Something teased her memory as she pursued her quarry. Often she was only able to see him because the tip of his bow stood out over the sea of heads bobbing up and down in front of her. The tickle in her brain grew increasingly annoying and her temper worse as the crowd steadily increased in size.

"Excuse me. Pardon me, please."

Her efforts at civility were wasted. Afraid that she would lose him, she began pushing her way through the crowd. She had almost caught up to him when the street opened up onto the fields set aside for the various competitions.

Standing on her toes, she tried to look above the people in front of her. It was no use. How could he have disappeared like that? Cursing in frustration, she moved with the crowd out onto the playing fields. The tickle in her mind remained. Why would such an unremarkable boy seem so familiar?

Off to the left two massive men greased in pig's fat tried to throw each other to the ground. The wrestling pit. Certainly not her favorite sport. Off to the right part of the field was set aside for the spear toss, and she assumed the boxing and quarterstaff contests took place in the rings next to it. She scanned the crowd, but with no luck. The boy was nowhere in sight. Not knowing what else to do, she headed for the archery contest remembering the bow across his back.

"Kaylie, over here."

Kaylie turned toward the voice and saw Lissa and Erinn. They had found a good spot right along one of the rails separating the target area from the spectators.

"We didn't expect you," said Erinn. "You wanted to see Ragin's shooting after all, yes?"

Kaylie ignored her friend's comment as the two giggled shrilly. If she rose to the bait, the teasing would never end.

"Where's Jenna?"

"She's on the other side," answered Lissa. Her voice turned hot and sultry. "She wanted to get as close to Berral as possible."

Both Lissa and Erinn laughed wickedly, but Kaylie wasn't really paying attention. Where could he have gone? She knew him, but from where?

She was certain she had met him before, but her memory was no help. Her lack of success was putting her in a particularly bad temper. Both Lissa and Erinn recognized the look and decided that their teasing should stop, at least for the time being. They focused their attention instead on some of the competitors. Kaylie followed their gaze.

About a hundred men stood in a line out on the field, with just as many targets made of wicker and hay opposite them. A cloth with a bull's-eye painted on it covered each target. Many of the archers were older, their greying hair and grizzled features telling of experience and skill. Probably soldiers, she guessed. Kaylie began running her eyes over each one when someone blocked her line of sight.

"I'm so glad you came, Kaylie. As I said before, my victory here today would mean nothing if you were not here to see it."

Ragin reached out for her hand, hoping to kiss it once more, but Kaylie expected the maneuver this time and withdrew her hands from the railing before he could take hold. Her reluctance did not put him off, however. He simply moved closer.

"Don't you think, Ragin, that before you claim victory, you should first take part in the contest? It looks like you might have some stiff competition," she said, motioning to the men on the other side of the railing.

Ragin snorted derisively and glanced behind his back at the other archers.

"I doubt they will offer me much in the way of competition. Maddan could probably beat this lot." Ragin leaned forward against the rail. "Perhaps a sweet kiss for luck?"

Ragin's eyes were more certain than hopeful — certain that Kaylie would accede to his wishes. He might expect such from others, but not from her.

"From your own words, I doubt you will need any luck today." Kaylie pulled back from the rail.

"Perhaps afterward, then," said Ragin, his smile now somewhat forced. He was not used to being refused.

"Archers to your station!"

A young man wearing the clothes of a courtier rode out onto the field on a white horse, his cockeyed hat flopping wildly on his head. On this afternoon he was the judge, rather than performing some menial task for a lord, and he planned to play his role to the hilt.

Ragin bowed slightly to Kaylie, then walked back onto the field to take his place among the others.

"Confident, isn't he?" said Lissa, who had stood there quietly, listening intently to Kaylie's conversation.

"Arrogant," grumbled Kaylie. She continued to sweep her eyes from archer to archer when her breath caught in her throat.

There he was, standing just a few places down from Ragin. He wasn't very tall, nor did he appear very imposing. Yet, there was something about him that made him stand out. Maybe it was his comfortable stance, the way he leaned against his bow. It seemed as if the bow were more a part of him rather than a tool for his use. His posture spoke of confidence and skill.

He was looking the other way when suddenly, as if he knew someone was watched him, his head whipped around. Their eyes locked together for an instant. Kaylie was shocked by the intensity of his gaze. His green eyes flashed brilliantly and within them lay recognition. She was right. They had met before. Then the wall that had blocked her memories crumbled. It was him! From the Burren and the hill. She knew it for a fact. There was no way to mistake his eyes.

"So who do you think will win?" asked Erinn. "Ragin?"

Kaylie looked over at her friend, a knowing smile on her face. "I doubt it. If I were you I'd pick the boy three places over."

"Him?" asked Erinn. "He probably can't even pull back his bow far enough to shoot an arrow."

"I've got five golds that say otherwise."

"You're on," said Erinn. "If you want to lose five golds so easily, that's fine by me. I'm putting my money on Ragin."

12

TEST OF CHARACTER

"**A**rchers, we will begin at 100 feet," announced the judge. The minor official pranced his horse down the line of contestants as he repeated himself so all could hear.

"You will have one shot each. If you miss the bull's-eye, you will withdraw from the line. After each shot the targets will be moved back twenty feet. You will shoot again. We will continue until there is but one left who has hit the bull's-eye. Good luck to you all." The courtier then trotted his horse behind the line of archers.

"Yes, good luck to you all," said Ragin to the men around him. "Though it will do you little good."

Several of the archers who heard his mocking comment grumbled under their breaths. Thomas simply ignored him, guessing that he had found the arrogant and intolerable Ragin. Thomas had arrived at the Festival in the early morning, leaving Beluil to wander the southern tip of Oakwood Forest. He marveled at all the strange sights and sounds, having never seen anything like it before. During the first hour he had wandered around in a daze, looking at everything at once.

Initially, he felt completely out of place. He was used to the rhythm of the forest, and the milling crowd made him distinctly uncomfortable. After a while, though, he got used to it and began to enjoy himself. He went from booth to booth, examining the jewelry and spices and fabrics and weapons and other trinkets, talking with the vendors and passersby and learning more of the goings on at the Festival.

While examining some of the blades in a blacksmith's shop he overheard the conversation of several men selecting steel arrow tips and discussing the upcoming archery contest. The conversation always came back to Ragin Tessaril, son of the High King. He had won the competition two years before, and rumor had it he hadn't stopped talking about it. Thomas quickly gathered that Ragin was not well loved, especially after learning how he enjoyed taunting and insulting his competitors.

After leaving the blacksmith's shop, Thomas wandered the Festival for a time deep in thought. He really wasn't supposed to be there, but he had assumed that if he kept to himself his presence would go unnoticed. However, the idea of taking part in an archery contest intrigued him. He rarely had the opportunity to match his skills against others.

Though Rynlin had told him he was a match for any Highlander, he had never had the chance to prove it to himself. He originally came to the Festival thinking that he might bump into the girl from the forest, assuming she would be there because her father would be. But once he saw how many people had come, he doubted that he would find her.

So why not have a little fun before going home? Then, much to his surprise, he had seen her. Or rather she had seen him. As he stood there waiting for the competition to begin, he scanned the onlookers, amazed that so many people came to watch. For a brief second, the hairs on the back of his neck stood on end, as if someone watched him.

Turning around he saw Kaylie standing by the railing, their

eyes meeting for a brief moment. He knew immediately that she recognized him, and that realization almost shattered his resolve. Butterflies suddenly hatched in his stomach and his arms and legs felt weak. She was more beautiful than he remembered.

He considered saying hello when reality struck full force and his fears rose to the surface. He wasn't supposed to be at the Festival, and now that he was, he should never have thought to take part in the archery competition. He should have remained in the background. He pulled his gaze away from those deep blue eyes, finding it hard to do.

As the men around him performed their last-second preparations, Thomas stood there calmly, his body sideways to the target, his feet spaced a comfortable distance apart. Closing his eyes briefly, he pushed all his thoughts to the back of his mind. The world around him gradually disappeared, until he was absolutely alone, except for his bow, arrow and the target.

"Archers, are you ready?" shouted the judge, who sat comfortably on his horse.

Thomas raised his bow and pulled back on the string in one smooth motion. Quiet draped itself around him. The buzz of the crowd, the play of the wind across the grass forgotten.

"Release!"

A swarm of arrows sped through the air toward the targets, almost of all of them settling in the cloth and hay with a loud thump. Thomas' arrow struck dead center, as did Ragin's. More than half of the competitors hit the bull's-eye in all. A squad of Dunmoorian soldiers ran out onto the field, knocking down the targets of the archers who missed and pulling the arrows out of the targets that struck true before dragging the hay and wicker structures back twenty feet.

"You did well on the first shot, gentlemen," said Ragin, using his bow as a staff as he waited for the next round. "Unfortunately, I'm virtually certain your luck will soon run out."

His words earned him several angry scowls, but he did not deign to notice them. He was the Prince of Armagh after all, and they all knew it. He could say or do almost anything he liked. One harsh word from one of the archers could lead to several unpleasant nights in the dungeon, or worse. The thin-skinned Prince's reputation was well known.

"Archers, are you ready?" shouted the judge again.

Thomas raised his bow and pulled back on the string until it was even with his cheek. Calm settled around him, as the grumbles of those archers already out of the competition washed over him with no real effect.

"Release!"

Arrows soared through the air, their steel tips striking home. The soldiers ran out onto the field and knocked down even more targets. Thomas hit dead center once again. He stood there calmly waiting for the next round. Ragin's taunts grew worse, earning himself even more angry grumbles from the remaining competitors.

The process continued for several more rounds. Each time the soldiers knocked down more targets as archers failed to hit the bull's-eye. Maddan and Ragin's other friends proved no match as the targets moved back, dropping out in the late rounds. Each time Ragin insulted his rivals and their skills, and each time Thomas ignored him, focusing on the task at hand, aware of only his bow, the arrow and the target. The targets were pulled back to three hundred feet and only a handful of archers remained. Thomas now stood the closest to Ragin, and thus drew his focus.

"You've done well so far, boy," said Ragin, eyeing Thomas' garb. "Where did you learn to shoot? Out in the forest with the squirrels?"

The Armaghian Prince laughed at his own joke, though he had no idea how close he had come to the truth. Thomas calmly examined the Prince of Armagh, taking in the arrogant stance and expression, clearly unimpressed by what he saw. Actually answering would only give Ragin more fuel for his comments. Instead, Thomas simply smiled before turning his attention back to his target. With his peripheral vision, he saw a brief flicker of irritation pass across Ragin's face.

"Archers, are you ready?"

The remaining archers raised their bows, strings taut, waiting for the command. The crowd was silent, caught up in the drama of the competition, bets going back and forth at a furious pace.

"Release!"

This time, of the five who remained, only two succeeded.

"So it comes down to a final shot," said Ragin, studying Thomas. There was nothing remarkable about him at all. Of all the archers who began the competition, Ragin never thought that he would have to contend with this boy for the prize. He had thought Berral of Benewyn stood the best chance of staying with him.

The soldiers finished their work, placing two targets at a distance of three hundred forty feet. The bull's-eyes were barely visible. The cheers of the crowd gradually quieted as the anticipation of what was to follow took control.

"Gentlemen, congratulations on making it to the final round," said the judge, walking his horse around Thomas and Ragin so the crowd could see and hear him as well. The competition was coming to an end and soon he would return to his normal routine, lost again in the constant shuffle of courtiers and other assistants. "We will apply slightly different rules at this stage. You will have five seconds to loose as many arrows as you can at your target. At the end of five seconds, the man with the most arrows in the bull's-eye wins. Do you understand?"

Thomas and Ragin nodded.

"Good luck to you then." The judge nudged his horse back

around the two archers, disappointed once more at having to exit the stage.

Looking out across the field at his target, Thomas judged how many arrows he could release in the allotted time. He then stuck the appropriate number of shafts point first into the ground so they would be within easy reach. Ragin did the same.

"Now, boy, you will see the difference between a peasant and a lord," said Ragin.

Thomas again examined the Prince of Armagh, smiling briefly before turning back to the targets. During his training in the circle, several of his opponents took much the same approach to combat as Ragin, hurling taunts and other barbs in an attempt to break his concentration. Thomas had learned the hard way that that was the quickest way to lose. He refused to allow a spoiled, arrogant bastard like Ragin do it to him now.

"Archers, are you ready?"

The judge's words rang out across the field. A hush fell over the crowd. For some it was simply the fun of the contest; for others, money.

"Release!"

Arrows sped through the air at a furious rate as the two made the most of their time. Thomas' motions were a blur as he released, pulled an arrow from the ground, nocked it to his bow, aimed, released, then went through the motions again and again. The rabid cheers of the crowd fell on deaf ears. At the moment, all Thomas heard was the twang of the string and the thump of the arrow as it hit home.

"Stop!"

The judge nudged his horse to a trot out onto the field so he could get a better look at the targets. The soldiers had already run out to count the number of arrows that had struck true.

"Better luck next time, boy," said Ragin, certain of his victory. His smile became a sneer. He had released three arrows in the five seconds, with two hitting the edge of the bull's-eye and a third close to the center. From this distance, it looked like Thomas had only managed to hit the bull's-eye once. "As I said before, an excellent test of lord and commoner."

Thomas ignored Ragin's jibe and instead glanced at the targets. Thomas knew the truth. He saw the judge talking with the soldiers, who gestured animatedly at Thomas' target. The judge rode slowly back across the field, appearing somewhat dazed. The crowd was silent, waiting for the news.

"What's your name, boy?" asked the judge, looking down at Thomas. The courtier's face was white, as if he had seen something he couldn't quite believe.

"Thomas."

"Thomas," said the judge, "you are hereby declared the best archer in the Eastern Kingdoms. Ten strikes in five seconds."

The judge spoke as if he still didn't quite believe it. A thunderous cheer erupted from the crowd, drowning out whatever else he had to say. Some cheered for Thomas' remarkable victory, others because Ragin had lost. The groans came from those who had bet against this unknown archer.

Every so often, Thomas could pick out a certain voice, and almost always it held the words, "Ten arrows? That's impossible!" Or "Did you see how fast he was shooting? I've never seen anything like it before!"

Butterflies danced in Thomas' stomach. Cool and confident while shooting, the recognition made him nervous. This certainly wasn't what he had in mind when arriving at the Festival. He had planned on a quiet excursion. If Rya and Rynlin saw him now, they'd— well, he really didn't want to think about it.

"What?" shouted Ragin in shock, unable to hide his anger. He ran out onto the field to get a better look, thinking the soldiers were wrong.

When he finally got to where he could clearly see the target, his mouth fell open in shock. What had looked like one arrow back at the shooting line was actually ten, yet they were spaced so closely together, the bolts were virtually indistinguishable except from a close distance. This was absolutely impossible! How could a commoner shoot—

"I was taught that there was no difference between a lord or a commoner," said Thomas, walking up behind Ragin. "Birth should not outweigh a man's character or actions. I see that those who taught me were wrong. Clearly there is a difference."

Ragin whipped around, his face an angry red because of the barb. Thomas' grin only increased his rage, yet before he could do anything, the crowd rushed forward to congratulate the new champion and take him up to the podium to collect his prize.

Ragin could only stand there and watch, powerless and mute. Losing to a commoner — a common boy no less — was bad enough, but having to bear his insults was something else entirely. He could do nothing about it now, but he would not soon forget.

13

REALIZATION

Kaylie watched the entire contest with rapt attention, unable to take her eyes from the boy with light brown hair and sparkling green eyes. The speed and grace with which he shot entranced her, bringing back memories of that horrible morning in Oakwood Forest. In fact, she had gotten so drawn into the contest, she had almost forgotten to breathe during the final round.

It had to be him. She would never forget what had happened only a few months before. Though she had not gotten a good look at her rescuer then because of the sun rising behind him, she was certain that she had found him. Thoughts of the Raptor immediately passed through her mind. Could the boy be the Raptor?

The stories she had heard about this almost mythical protector of the forest seemed preposterous, but this boy's latest display eliminated the last of her doubts. She quickly concluded as well that this was the mysterious archer on the hill who had saved her, the only thing missing being his large black wolf.

But how could it be? This boy, this Thomas, looked to be no

older than she. He didn't have a particularly large build, and he was no taller than she, though his strength was obvious since he pulled back on his large bow with ease. There was nothing distinct about him, except for his eyes. She smiled to herself as the crowd ducked under the railing to congratulate the new Champion Archer of the Eastern Kingdoms.

He obviously had a ready wit if he had so successfully insulted Ragin, as seemed to be the case by Ragin's sour, almost murderous, expression. Kaylie had not been able to single out what had bothered her about Ragin before. While watching Thomas, she had found it — his arrogance and conceit, the way he held himself above everyone else, as if no one was his equal. When she looked at Thomas, all she saw was a quiet confidence. He didn't brag or boast, instead letting his actions speak for his abilities. Unable to take her eyes off of him, she ducked under the railing as well, leaving Lissa and Erinn.

Her face grew determined. She would find this Thomas and confirm her suspicions about him. She had to know if she was right.

14

WHISPERED PRAISE

Thomas didn't know what to do when he was hoisted onto the shoulders of some of the onlookers and carried to the podium. It all happened in a blur as the crowd roared its approval when the judge presented the prize money for winning the archery contest. Thomas just dropped it in his pocket as several of the archers and other well-wishers came up to slap him on the back and congratulate him.

More than once he heard whispered praise of how nice it was to see someone of common stock better one of noble. Thomas' original estimate was correct. No one here had much love for Ragin Tessaril, and his defeat made Thomas' victory all the sweeter for them.

Almost an hour had passed before the flow of people coming up to the podium stopped and Thomas was finally able to leave. He had scanned the faces approaching him several times, looking for Kaylie, but to no avail. He had seen her talking to Ragin before the contest began, so there was little reason for him to think that she would be here now. She was a princess, after all.

Oh well. It would have been nice to see her again, to actually talk to her. Just thinking about her made his heart beat a little faster. Sighing in resignation, Thomas jumped down from the podium, bow across his shoulder and his arrows back safely in his quiver thanks to one of the other archers who retrieved them for him.

He started to make his way back toward the Festival booths. It was time for him to go. He had come here hoping to be a nobody and now his name was on everyone's lips. If Rya found out about this, she'd throw a fit. And then Rynlin would not be happy with him either. Whenever Rya got angry, Rynlin heard about it, and usually more than he wanted.

15

FORMAL INTRODUCTION

Kaylie waited in frustration along the edges of the crowd that swarmed Thomas after his victory. After a few efforts to push her way through, she realized she'd never get close enough to him while he was on the podium.

"Are you all right, Kaylie?" asked Lissa, who finally caught up with her. "You look put out."

Kaylie stood there with her arms crossed and one foot tapping.

"I'm fine," she snapped. She hated waiting. "Where's Erinn? She owes me five golds."

"I'm afraid you'll have to collect from her later. We ran into Jenna and Berral. A friend of Berral's caught Erinn's eye. I'm afraid we're on our own for now."

Kaylie grunted noncommittally, not really listening to Lissa. The crowd was finally thinning out. Perhaps she could reach the podium now.

"Ragin, Maddan and the others are heading back to the castle now," said Lissa, her eyes dancing with mischief. Kaylie was obviously interested in this champion archer, yet Lissa chose not to say anything. She had known Kaylie for quite a long time and recognized her moods well. Now was not the time to tease her. "Would you like to come with us?"

"No. I think I'd like to see more of the Festival first. If you see my father, just tell him I'll be back later this afternoon." Kaylie continued to watch the crowd, looking for a chance to get to the podium.

"All right," said Lissa, a knowing smile on her face. She pushed her way back through the mass of people blocking her way to the castle. "Good hunting."

Kaylie whipped around, looking for Lissa. Just what did she mean by that? Unable to pick her out of the crowd, she turned back to the podium. Wait. Where did he go? She'd only turned her head for a moment and now he was gone. Blast that Lissa! She always knew how to irritate her, and now she might have lost him because of her. Thankfully the crowd had diminished, so she had a much easier time reaching the podium. Unfortunately, Thomas had already left.

Jumping onto the stand, she spun around. There! He was heading back to the Festival. He was hard to pick out, but the large bow slung across his back gave him away. She leapt down and ran after him, or at least tried to. Every time she thought she gained on him, someone stepped in her way and slowed her down.

She looked for him again. There! Just ahead of her. She dodged through the crowd, trying to catch up. She was about to reach for his shoulder when he disappeared. What the— He was right there! She stopped and stamped her foot on the ground in irritation. This was unfair. How could he disappear like that so quickly?

"You are extremely persistent." The voice came from right behind her.

Kaylie jumped around, her heart in her throat.

"You have no right sneaking up on me like that," she said heatedly, her eyes blazing. Of course, she conveniently failed to mention that she had been trying to sneak up on him. "Scaring young women is not exactly appropriate behavior."

She wanted to say more, but found that she couldn't. The whole time she was talking, he stared directly into her eyes. It made her feel as if they were the only two people there at the moment, rather than being two in the middle of several thousand. His brilliant green eyes entranced her. There was a sparkle there she found irresistible.

"I believe you've been stalking me for the better part of the morning," he said, an easy smile on his face that warmed the hard edge of his eyes. There was humor there, as well as an uncommon seriousness, and something else she couldn't put her finger on. The person standing across from her couldn't be much older than her, she confirmed. In fact, he looked quite young except for his eyes. "Although I'm not an expert in courtly behavior, I didn't think spying was taught to young ladies, and especially princesses."

"Just how do you know I'm a princess?" she retorted. She had made it a point of not dressing like one, wanting to blend into the crowd.

Abruptly he started walking toward the Festival. Kaylie hurried to catch up. "It wasn't hard to figure out."

He was nervous. That's what she had seen in his eyes but couldn't determine at first. But why would he be nervous? Wait a second. Maybe she made him nervous. Kaylie smiled at her sudden understanding, pleased by her realization.

"You remember me, I see." They entered the Festival grounds again, passing by several persistent hawkers they ignored. "I can tell by the look in your eyes."

"Yes," replied Kaylie, grinning from cheek to cheek. She enjoyed nothing so much in life as being right. "I do remember you. From the waterfall in the Burren and then again in Oakwood Forest with the Fearhounds."

She watched him out of the corner of her eye for a moment, her thoughts jumbled. She wanted to say how heroic he had been for saving her life twice, and her father's life, about how magnificent he had appeared up on the hill, shooting down at the Fearhounds unafraid during their charge. Yet, such words didn't feel right. Then she remembered how disappointed she had been when he had disappeared into the forest without saying a word.

"Thank you. You never stayed around long enough for me to say that either time."

There was a rebuke in Kaylie's words, but Thomas either missed it or ignored it.

"I heard it the first time," he said, not looking at her directly. It seemed as if he was going to say more, then chose not to. Kaylie smiled with pleasure. He was nervous. It made her feel good to know that she could do that to someone, and not because she was a princess.

The fact that she was a princess made most people nervous, though she had gotten used to it. She had even learned how to make people more comfortable, or uncomfortable, as the circumstances warranted. No, he wasn't nervous because she was a princess. He was nervous because she was a woman. She relished the thought.

"When Fearhounds attack a few sometimes hang back to pursue any prey that might escape the pack," said Thomas. "I wanted to make sure there weren't any lurking about."

Kaylie looked at him in amazement. She was slightly piqued because he had such a good excuse, but what really surprised her was the nonchalant way he had said it. But there was not a trace of conceit or arrogance in his voice. It was purely a statement of fact, as if killing Fearhounds was an everyday task for him, much like a blacksmith reshaping a horseshoe. Except the horseshoe wouldn't hunt you down and sink finger-long teeth into your neck.

Kaylie shuddered at the image she created in her mind. This boy really was quite remarkable, and he certainly was full of surprises. Kaylie wanted to get some answers to her questions. He was clearly flustered and did not like talking about himself, so she tried a different tack.

"You know, I don't think we've ever been properly introduced," she said. "My name's Kaylie."

"I know," he said, stopping so that they once again stood face to face.

For some reason Kaylie was pleased that he already knew her name. He remained silent for quite awhile, standing there looking at her. It was as if he was memorizing every tiny little detail of her face — the curve of her chin, the length of her eyelashes, the few freckles on her nose. His eyes sparkled with delight, their deep green color — almost a glow she realized — capturing her again.

For a moment, her knees felt weak and she was afraid she was going to fall down. Now why was that happening? She had heard from her friends how certain boys made them weak in the knees, like Jenna with Berral, but this obviously couldn't be the same thing. Maybe she was ill. She had skipped lunch, so that was probably it. She was only curious about him, not infatuated like Jenna was with Berral. Her thoughts strengthened her resolve, and her knees.

"Kaylie," he said finally, almost savoring her name. She liked the way he said it. "It's a pleasure to meet you."

He took her hand and kissed her knuckles, much like any gentleman would upon meeting a lady. As his lips touched her skin her heart almost stopped.

"My name is Thomas. Would you like to join me for lunch?" Thomas' heart skipped a beat, fearful that she would say no.

"Yes, that would be nice," she said, allowing herself to be directed toward a stand selling an assortment of hot pastries and other treats. The whole way there she played with his name in her mind. Thomas. Yes, that was a good name for him. A strong name. A name that seemed to fit him perfectly.

16

LEARNING MORE

"So where's your friend?"

"My friend?" asked Thomas.

They had found a small copse of trees just outside the Festival grounds. The long grass offered a comfortable seat and the warm sun fended off the chill of the day.

"Yes, your friend. The wolf, remember? He's hard to forget."

Kaylie could still visualize the wolf from the last time she saw him. He was as large as the Fearhounds, and seemed even more ferocious. His black fur matched with his large white teeth made for a terrifying sight indeed.

"Beluil."

Thomas hungrily bit into his lunch, enjoying the venison and gravy hidden within the pastry shell. They had bought lunch at a stall run by an extremely large woman who obviously enjoyed the food she cooked. They had decided that if she liked it so much, so would they.

"He's around somewhere." Kaylie looked around quickly, a frightened look in her eyes. Thomas was quick to reassure her. "Don't worry. He's harmless. He spends most of his time trying to get his belly rubbed. Not what you would expect from a man-eating wolf, now, is it?"

Kaylie chuckled at the image that popped into her mind — the large wolf lying on its back and sighing with pleasure as Thomas scratched his stomach.

"So how is it that you two are friends? I've never heard of such a thing. In fact, most people would not only run away from—"

"Beluil."

"—Beluil, but also from you. They would think you could work Dark Magic or were possessed by evil spirits."

She laughed nervously at the thought. She really didn't know him very well at all. A whisper in the back of her mind asked what if she was right. How else could he learn to use a bow so well?

"I see your point. Most people fear what they don't understand."

Thomas licked gravy off his fingers, having finished the pastry. His stomach full, he leaned back on an elbow and stretched out his legs. At first, Thomas' stomach did somersaults as he talked with Kaylie. He didn't know what to say. Not because she was a princess, but because she was a girl. The last time he had talked with a girl his own age was back at the Crag.

To make the situation even more difficult, he was experiencing certain feelings toward her that he had never felt. It was all extremely confusing to him. With time, though, his nervousness subsided. He soon found that talking with Kaylie was not only easy, but also fun.

"Beluil and I have been friends for a long time, in fact we grew up together, so it's a very long story. The short of it is that we were both thrust into the same sort of situation and we've been together ever since."

"Is he somewhere close by? I'd love to meet him. I thanked you for what you did for us, but I never thanked him."

Kaylie looked around hopefully. The idea of petting an extremely large and dangerous-looking black wolf appealed to her. Her blood started to flow a little faster in her veins. She had wanted excitement and adventure, and now she just might get it.

"He's in Oakwood Forest right now, probably looking for an attractive female wolf," laughed Thomas. "I'll pass on your thanks, though."

"Thank you. Please do."

Kaylie studied Thomas for a moment, taking in his hair, his face, his smile. There was so much she wanted to learn about him, but she didn't know where to begin. Her stomach fluttered every time he glanced at her. It must have been the pastry. The meat had been just a little too spicy. It couldn't have been anything else, could it?

"How did you learn to shoot the bow?" Kaylie sat cross-legged in the grass, her elbows on her knees and chin perched in her hands.

Thomas studied Kaylie for several seconds, wondering whether to tell her the truth. He doubted, however, that she would believe that he learned from the spirit of the greatest archer ever to walk the continent. Besides, he still had to exercise caution. His grandparents had counseled caution ever since he was a boy, and now was not the time to give in to recklessness, even when being questioned by someone with such a pretty face.

"From a friend," he replied. "He made me practice until I got it right."

Kaylie waited expectantly for Thomas to say more, but he didn't, much to her annoyance. Unsuccessful with that approach, she tried a different tack.

"So where are you from?"

"From the east," Thomas answered vaguely.

"From around Fal Carrach? Or Benewyn? Or maybe the Highlands?" Kaylie was not one to give up easily.

"From the east," repeated Thomas.

He smiled when he saw Kaylie frown. She was used to having her questions answered. He decided to ask some of his own and perhaps turn her mind to other things.

"So who were those two girls standing with you at the railing?"

A sudden burst of jealousy erupted within Kaylie. Why would Thomas want to know about them? Wait a second. Why should she be jealous? She pushed her emotions away. She was just talking to him, that's all. It probably wasn't jealousy anyway. She just didn't like it when people dodged her questions. She didn't like it at all. Yes, that was probably the cause of her irritation.

"The blond one was Lissa, and the other Erinn. We grew up together in the Rock. Why do you ask?"

Yes, it must be her anger at him avoiding her questions. That was the only explanation for the tightness in her voice.

"Just curious. They seemed to be quite interested in Ragin."

"Yes, well, they're both very much interested in good looks," she said, her voice scornful.

"And you're not?" Thomas sounded quite doubtful.

"No, I'm not," said Kaylie, leaning back in the grass on her elbows. "Ragin is good looking, I will admit. But to be honest, there's something about him that seems off."

"A lot of people seem to have the same perspective."

"Oh?" Kaylie wasn't really surprised to hear that.

"Yes, many of the archers were none too pleased by his boasting during the tournament. I take it he's not very well liked?"

"No, he's not very well liked at all," answered Kaylie. "But he and his father don't really care. All they want is to be feared. It's the way Armagh is ruled. So long as they are feared, they believe they are safe."

"A very astute observation," said Thomas. "I could understand now why Ragin was so upset at losing."

"Yes, he wasn't happy, was he?" laughed Kaylie, enjoying the memory of Ragin's failure. "That was part of it, you know. You weren't afraid of him. That probably annoyed him more than the fact that you beat him. By the way, what did you say to him after you won? He looked like he wanted to stick a sword in you."

"If we were alone he probably would have tried," agreed Thomas, smiling as he remembered how his words affected the High Prince. With his beet red face and flaring nostrils, Ragin resembled a volcano ready to explode. "I didn't really say anything at all. I was just correcting something he had told me earlier. Obviously, he didn't appreciate it."

Thomas' expression came across as innocent, but his eyes shined with mischief.

"I guess you could say I was rubbing it in." Thomas held out his hands in mock supplication. "I know, I know. It's not very honorable. I just couldn't resist."

"I wouldn't worry too much over it. He certainly deserved it."

"Yes, he did," said Thomas, a satisfied smile on his face. "So, besides politics, what are some of your other interests, Kaylie?"

"My interests?"

Thomas' question took her by surprise, never having been asked the question before. She really didn't know how to answer. Most people simply assumed that she had no time to do anything else but act like a princess. She was often seen as a way to gain something, and not as an actual person.

"Yes, your interests. What do you like to do besides discuss politics?"

"Well, right now I'm learning how to fight with a sword."

"Really," said Thomas, sitting up. "Are you any good?"

His voice didn't hold the derision that she had come to expect from people like Ragin and Maddan, who scoffed at her efforts, but rather true interest. Speaking with Thomas was becoming an extremely enjoyable experience. She couldn't remember the last time someone had treated her like a regular person, rather than as a princess.

"Kael Bellilil, our Swordmaster, says I am," she replied with pride, though careful not to brag. It was obvious that Thomas had no use for such talk.

"I still have a lot more to learn, though. I didn't realize how heavy a sword was until I started. I'm actually better with a dagger. For the longest time my father wouldn't let me practice the sword, so I learned the dagger instead. In fact, my father didn't give in until after the attack in Oakwood Forest. It was not the way I wanted to convince him, but at least something good came from that experience."

"Well, if the Swordmaster says you're good with a blade, I'm sure you are." Kael Bellilil. That was a Highland name, and one that sounded familiar to him. "Of course, you can't spend all your time in the training circle."

"No, I don't," said Kaylie, with some disappointment. She wished she could spend much more time there, but her duties, and her father, wouldn't allow it. "I also do things with my friends. I don't lead a very exciting life like you do, though. If I'm not in the training circle, then I'm learning to be a queen."

"Well, I really wouldn't call my life exciting."

"Oh, come now." Kaylie leaned forward again. "Fighting a pack of Fearhounds isn't exciting?" she asked sarcastically. "What else do you do in the forest?"

"Whatever's necessary, really."

Kaylie looked at Thomas in obvious frustration. No matter how hard she tried, she could barely get anything out of him. His answers, though truthful, were remarkably evasive. She considered asking him point blank if he was the Raptor, then decided against it.

"It must be a lot of fun to wander through the forest every day, looking for new things to do, finding adventure behind every tree," she said. "Fearhounds one day, who knows what the next."

"It's not really like that," protested Thomas. "I don't go looking for trouble."

It wasn't the complete truth, Thomas admitted to himself, but there were certain things he didn't want Kaylie to know. At least not yet. Besides, he really didn't go looking for trouble. Trouble simply had a habit of finding him.

"Even so, most of the time I'm cooped up in a castle going from one stupid ceremony or audience to the next or making decisions about the most inconsequential things. It's a complete waste of time, really. Nothing I do is important."

Even to Kaylie her words sounded somewhat childish, though she chose to ignore that fact. Her face scrunched up into a look of distaste. Her life wasn't what she wanted it to be, and now was as good a time as any to sulk.

Thomas leaned forward and captured Kaylie's eyes. He wanted to make sure that she remembered what he had to say.

"You think I don't have responsibilities, but I do. I have a great many responsibilities. It's really just a question of how you look at things."

"What do you mean?"

"Give me an example of one of the decisions you've made, one of the most inconsequential." Thomas' tone indicated that he didn't think her decisions could ever be unimportant.

Kaylie thought for a moment. "Well, a few weeks ago a woman came to the Crag complaining that a craftsman had sold her a shoddy teakettle and refused to repair it."

"And what did you do?"

"I looked at the teakettle and couldn't see anything wrong

with it. But the woman said that when you poured water into it, the teakettle leaked. So I had a guard do that, and it leaked. It was a trivial thing, really." Kaylie clearly didn't understand why Thomas was so interested in a teakettle.

"What did you do next?"

Why he was so intrigued with her story?

"Well, I had the craftsman brought to the Rock. I had him give the woman back her money and then fined him two golds for doing such a poor job. He also had to fix the teakettle for her."

"And you don't think that's important?"

"Not really. It was just a teakettle that cost no more than a few coppers. How could it be important?"

"It's all a matter of perspective. To you, a few coppers is nothing. But to that woman, she may have saved her money for weeks to buy that teakettle. Imagine her dismay to find that after all that hard work, in a sense someone had stolen her money."

"I never thought of it like that." Why didn't she?

"Why should you? You've never had to do that before. Not only did the woman get her hard-earned money back, but you also helped everyone else in the same situation as the woman."

"What do you mean by that?"

"Well, now everyone who buys something in the market-place knows that if there's a legitimate problem with it, and the craftsman or merchant won't make amends, they can come to you for an equitable solution. And the craftsmen and merchants know that if they don't do good work, or sell a quality product, they'll be fined, giving them added incentive to do the job right."

"I never thought of it like that before."

"It's just a matter perspective," repeated Thomas, pleased by her reaction. "What you see as responsibility is really an opportunity. Why do you think your father has you make those decisions?"

"He says it's so I'll be ready to rule Fal Carrach."

"He's not telling you everything, you know," said Thomas with a sly smile. "What you see as a burden he sees as a lesson. Your decisions are affecting people's lives, and though the decisions may not be important to you, they are extremely important to them. Maybe you should think of this responsibility as an opportunity."

"How so?"

"This is your chance to find out more about your people, and for your people to find out more about you. When the time comes for you to make decisions that can have a huge effect on their lives, they'll have confidence in you because they know you have sound judgment. You can find out what your people's hopes and dreams are, their fears and concerns. Don't waste the opportunity you have here. Your father's right. You'll be a queen one day, and a good one, I'm sure, if you listen to your people."

Kaylie stared in Thomas in shock, not expecting a lesson during their picnic. This champion archer was one surprise after another.

"And just how does someone who spends all of his time in the forest know so much?"

"I had very good teachers," answered Thomas with an impish grin.

Kaylie decided that it was time to change the subject. So far, despite her best efforts, they had spent most of their time together talking about her.

"So what's it like wandering around in the forest?"

Thomas settled back on his hands. "It's fun, exciting. I see something new every day. In a very real sense it feels like home." Thomas' voice was wistful for a moment. "I've never really felt comfortable behind stone walls. The trees give me all the security I need."

Thomas saw the way Kaylie was hanging on his every word. He could sympathize with her plight.

"You don't have a lot of fun at the Rock, do you?"

Kaylie sighed in frustration, remembering all the times she had wanted to go out into the countryside, or just to the shops in Ballinasloe, to do anything but what she had to do.

"No, not really."

"Why are you so interested in the forest?"

"For the same reason you are." Kaylie understood now why it was so easy to talk to Thomas. In many ways, they were very much alike. "It gives me a chance to escape. When I'm in the forest, I'm no longer a princess. It's nice not having those responsibilities for a time."

Thomas grinned, knowing exactly what she meant.

"Well, when you're in the forest, what do you see? What do you feel?"

"I see trees and bushes and plants and squirrels and birds." She didn't see the point to his question. "What do you mean what do I feel? Like I said, I feel free in a sense—"

"No, no. Sorry, I wasn't clear." Thomas paused for a moment, thinking of a better way to phrase his question. "When you're in the forest, do you feel as if you belong? As if you're a part of the forest?"

"I don't know," she replied. "I'm still not sure what you're asking."

"Come on," Thomas said, rising from his seat in the grass. He walked to the center of the glade in which they sat. Kaylie followed after him. "If I tried to explain it to you, it could take days. It's better to show you. You see, the forest is alive."

"I know the forest is alive," responded Kaylie, somewhat tartly.

"Let me explain," said Thomas, not rising to the bait. "The

forest is alive, but it's more alive than you think. It's a living, breathing thing. Just like you and me, really. And there's a power in it that only a handful of people can harness."

"Why so few?"

"I'm not really sure," answered Thomas. He smiled. He had asked the same question when Rynlin had lectured on the very same topic. "My grandparents say that almost anyone can to varying degrees. They simply haven't tried or don't want to. For the people strongest in this ability, it is obviously easier for them; for those not as strong, with time and the lack of use, their ability to harness this power gradually dissipates."

"Can I harness this power?" Kaylie asked, excitement in her voice.

"Perhaps," said Thomas. "We'll find out. Now look around you and tell me what you see."

Kaylie glanced at Thomas with a question in her eyes, then slowly spun around, taking in everything around her.

"I see the trees and bushes, of course. The squirrels and birds. The earth. The bird's nest on that branch over there. The brackenberry bushes." She wasn't sure if she had answered correctly.

"Good," said Thomas. "Yet everything you described is just a fraction of what's going on around you. You saw, but you really didn't see. Let me show you what I mean."

Thomas closed his eyes for a moment. It was hard to concentrate with Kaylie standing right next to him. Every time he looked at her his heart beat a little faster. In a flash the Talent flowed within him.

"Are you ready, Kaylie?"

Kaylie glanced at Thomas with complete trust in her eyes, and something more though she refused to admit it. The way he said her name sent a tingle through her body. She nodded in anticipation.

"Then give me your hand."

At first she couldn't tell if anything was happening when she felt the warmth of his touch, then in an instant it was like she had pushed through an invisible wall she had never known existed. A scarf had been pulled from her eyes. She gazed around the woods in wonder. Instead of seeing just the trees, she could actually feel their age and knowledge. That one, to her right, a huge silver maple, had been in this particular place for almost two hundred years, and that one next to it just a few years longer.

She could sense the sap running beneath the bark, and pick out the tiny ants using its rough exterior as a road in their constant search for food. Turning to the bird's nest she realized that several eggs lay there, and that from them two male and two female chicks would hatch. She couldn't explain how she knew, but she was certain of it. She examined the earth and realized that a mole lived just beneath her feet and that a small underground stream ran through the copse just off to her left.

She turned to look at Thomas, a huge smile on her face, then abruptly realized that she was no longer holding his hand. Losing her concentration, her dazzling new awareness disappeared.

"Was I doing that myself?" she asked, her face flushed with excitement. "After you let go of my hand?"

"Yes, you were," answered Thomas. "In the end whatever you saw was because of you."

"Is it magic?" she asked in a hushed whisper. Her voice grew more worried. "Dark Magic?"

She had heard stories of the evil done by warlocks who used Dark Magic, a power given to them by the Shadow Lord. Was she one of them? Was that why she could do this? Fear crept onto her face.

"A form of magic, yes. But not Dark Magic." Thomas sensed her concern. "Dark Magic can only be gained from the Shadow Lord, and to obtain it you have to pledge your soul to him. I'm assuming that you haven't done that?" Thomas raised a quizzical eyebrow.

"I most certainly have not," protested Kaylie.

"Then you have nothing to worry about," laughed Thomas. "As I said, almost everyone has some type of magic within them that can bring them closer to nature. Yours is obviously still with you. If you practice, you will grow more skilled in its use."

"Can you show me how?"

"Certainly," replied Thomas, glad that he would be able to spend more time with her. "When circumstances permit. Right now, though, we should probably head back. We've been away for quite a long time and your father probably will be worried."

Kaylie sighed in disappointment, wanting to stay longer but knowing that Thomas was correct. Still, her smile remained. The thrill of what she had just accomplished — all on her own — surged within her.

"How long will it take for me to learn how to do this without your help?"

"It depends," said Thomas, shrugging his shoulders. "You'll probably pick it up very quickly. But, if you want me to teach you, you'll have to promise me one thing."

"What's that?" she asked, suddenly wary.

"That you keep it to yourself. As I said before, not many people know of this particular ability, and most normally react with concern, even fear. I don't think you'd want them to call you a warlock. I know I certainly don't want that to happen. I've gotten into enough trouble already."

"It'll just be our secret, then," she said.

Having something to share with Thomas in private appealed to Kaylie. She latched onto his last comment? What kind of trouble might he be referring to?

"Good. Then let's head back to the Festival."

They exited the small copse of trees with Kaylie looking back in delight. This was the most fun and excitement she had experienced in— well, she couldn't remember when. And she could do magic! She could! All thanks to Thomas, of course. She had the sudden urge to hold his hand, and began to reach for it. She abruptly pulled her hand back before he noticed, uncertain of how he would react. She didn't want to risk spoiling such a wonderful afternoon. As she walked across the field toward the Festival, she realized she had not learned as much about him as she wished.

"Thomas, do you mind if I ask you a question?"

"Not at all," he replied with a smile.

Yet, as she looked at him, Kaylie saw the seriousness that never left his eyes. There might be a certain mischievousness there, as well as other emotions such as anger, but there was always a seriousness that she didn't think ever left those eyes. She was determined to find out the reason for that, but now was not the time. Instead, she had a more pressing question. One that she had wanted to ask since she had first run into him those many years before.

"Why did you help me in the Burren? You put yourself in grave danger, but I doubt you even thought twice about it."

He shrugged, unsure of how to reply.

"Please, Thomas. I really would like to know." And give me a real answer this time, she wanted to add.

Kaylie's beauty again swept him away as he gazed at her. Why did he help her? She was right. He had never thought twice about it, though he probably should have.

"It was a matter of responsibility. Just as you were explaining some of your responsibilities, I too have my own. The simple fact is that you needed help, so I gave it."

"You state it so simply, yet it is not a simple thing," said Kaylie, gazing at him as if she were trying to pierce his defenses. "If nothing else, you must give me the opportunity to repay you."

"And just what do you suggest, Kaylie?"

"I suggest a picnic," said Kaylie. "I'll meet you here tomorrow at noon."

Thomas looked at the beautiful girl standing before him for a long moment. He was supposed to return to the Isle of Mist tomorrow. Yet the idea of spending one more day with Kaylie was too irresistible to give up.

"I'll be here."

The smile that lit up Kaylie's face almost weakened his knees.

17

AN OPPORTUNITY

Ragin waited several minutes for Thomas and Kaylie to leave before moving from behind his tree. Not desiring the company of others, he had stormed off from the festival. And not wanting to have to deal with the anger of his father at his loss, his natural course had taken him to the woods just beyond the contest grounds.

As luck would have it, he had been in the right place at the right time. He had only heard bits and pieces of their conversation, but enough to know that an opportunity had fallen into his lap — a very large opportunity. He smiled wickedly. If he handled things well, he had much to gain, a scheme already forming in his mind. Now all he had to do was pull it off.

18

SAFE

They walked back to the Festival in silence after that, each consumed by their own thoughts. On the outside, Thomas' response to her question appeared simple. Yet Kaylie knew better. There was a complexity within her new friend that was hard to comprehend. She promised herself that eventually she would breach Thomas' defenses and discover what lay behind his constant wariness. They had just reached the outer edge of stalls when a terrible roar carried over the noises of the crowd. Thomas immediately ran toward it, a hard expression on his face, Kaylie right on his heels.

"Thomas!" she yelled.

She followed after him in a rush, shocked by his speed. There was no way he was going to get away from her so easily, she vowed to herself.

Thomas ran with little care for what was in front of him, forcing people to move out of his way. Some opened their mouths to protest, but upon seeing his murderous glare, wisely chose to remain silent. Kaylie was just quick enough to stay with him before the crowd closed back up again after Thomas' passage.

Kaylie almost slammed into Thomas' back when he slid to a halt in the loose dirt. He had stopped in front of a ramshackle stand, one of its two support beams holding up a large placard that bent precariously to one side. It was clearly ready to snap in two at any moment. The sign read "Falsuto, Dealer in Exotic Animals," yet just exactly what an exotic animal might be she wasn't sure. Another roar shattered the rhythm of the Festival. Kaylie found the source to her left.

Off to one side of the wobbly sign a huge bear rose up on its hind legs in anger, its massive claws tearing the air in front of it. The huge animal cried out in fury, allowing the crowd that had gathered around it to see its large, white teeth. A single swipe from one of those paws would easily tear a man in two. The people in the first few rows of the crowd shuffled back in fear from the angry bear, despite the thick steel chain attaching a collar around the animal's neck to a large stake driven into the ground, thereby preventing the bear from going where it wanted — after the man holding the whip.

"Don't worry, friends," said a rather large man whose belly greatly outsized any of his other features. His scraggly beard and sweat-streaked face gave him a dirty appearance. Kaylie assumed that this was Falsuto. "This beast isn't going anywhere. As I said before, I captured him at the edge of the Highlands single-handedly. He truly is a magnificent animal, is he not?"

Falsuto was not about to let the crowd answer. He had waited for quite some time before beginning the show, until several lords and ladies had wandered close by. The price he was asking for the bear could only be met by people of wealth, people who looked for unique things to make their friends jealous. He sensed that those people had arrived.

"Whether alive or stuffed, this magnificent specimen will fill your friends with envy and enemies with fear."

Falsuto knew his buyers quite well. The greed and one-upmanship was clear in the expressions of the lords and ladies present, and already they examined one another to judge their competition. Yes, he had timed it perfectly. Someone in this crowd would pay well for the bear, and Falsuto's whipping the animal into a frenzied anger had probably earned him a few hundred more golds than he normally would have gotten. Falsuto raised the whip above his head. One last crack should be just enough to start the bidding.

Thomas stood in the back of the crowd, his face turning white with anger. As the fat man raised the whip above his head again, Thomas lunged forward, knocking the people in front of him out of his way. Kaylie reached for Thomas' arm, but in vain.

Falsuto brought his arm down quickly, expecting to hear the sharp crack of the tip against the bear's back. Instead, sharp gasps of surprise echoed through the crowd. He felt the whip yanked from his grasp.

Thomas stared at Falsuto with anger-filled eyes, the whip firmly in his grasp. The dealer stepped back until the crowd impeded his progress. He didn't want to have anything to do with the green flames dancing there. The crowd watched this strange boy intently; some with fear, some with curiosity. Most expected the rage-filled bear to tear him apart, as the boy was within easy reach of those sharp, curved claws.

"Do not fear, my friend," said Thomas, turning toward the now strangely docile animal. The bear went down to four legs and rubbed his head against Thomas' shoulder in friendship. The ferocity had disappeared, replaced by trust. "You will be free."

The crowd stood mesmerized by the display, waiting anxiously to see what would happen next. To Kaylie, it seemed as if a hush had fallen over the entire Festival. She couldn't believe her eyes. Thomas had walked right up to a bear that easily weighed several thousand pounds, if not more, with absolutely no fear. And even more remarkable, the bear accepted him as a friend. Who was he? Was he really the Raptor? Her curiosity demanded that she find out.

Thomas turned his blazing eyes on Falsuto. "I do not approve of those who sell animals for sport or display. And I particularly dislike those who torture animals. I see that you do both."

Falsuto tried to step away from those fiery green eyes, yet he had nowhere to go with the crowd packed tight behind him. This had become too good a show for anyone to leave. Thomas looked down at the whip he now held.

"Perhaps you would like to know what it feels like."

Fear surged within Falsuto as he realized what this strange boy meant. His mouth suddenly dry from fear, he failed to respond.

"I thought not," said Thomas contemptuously.

Thomas flung the whip to the ground in disgust and walked over to the rundown stall, rummaging through several wood boxes until he found what he wanted. The bear waited calmly for his return. Taking hold of the chain, Thomas lifted the links onto the head of the steel stake, then swung down with the spiked hammer he had pulled out of a box. The chain shattered with a single stroke. The crowd gasped in fear, inching backward ever so slowly. The beast now loose, freed by this boy.

"You can't do that!" yelled Falsuto shrilly. He had still not found his voice, but at least he could speak again. "That's my bear!"

The bulky man fumbled at his side, trying to find the hilt of the sword that hung at his hip, but having a hard time because of the many folds of fat that hung over his belt.

Thomas stared at the man with cold eyes. "If you draw your sword, it is the last thing you will ever do."

Thomas' voice was filled with a cold certainty. Falsuto immediately dropped his arms to his sides. Pulling the purse that he had won in the archery contest from his pocket, Thomas threw it at the man's feet.

"For your trouble. I suggest you choose another occupation, Falsuto. If I see you selling animals again, I will test that whip on you next time."

Falsuto gulped in fear, yet was greedy enough to take his eyes off Thomas and the bear for a few seconds to reach down and grab the bag of gold coins. It disappeared in one of his many pockets.

Thomas looked at the crowd a final time, making sure that no one intended to interfere, before he and the bear walked past the broken-down booth and toward the trees at the edge of the Festival. The bear walked slowly beside him, its head right up against his side. The animal was tired and hurt and was not about to let his new friend out of his sight.

Kaylie watched the whole thing in amazement. Yet, strange as it may be, seeing the bear walking beside Thomas seemed right to her, though she couldn't figure out why. Thomas turned around quickly when they reached the trees and smiled at her, a smile which she returned, and then he disappeared into the forest, the bear trudging along at his side.

The crowd stood still for a moment longer before breaking out into a gaggle of excited whispers, still unable to believe their eyes. Kaylie knew that the story would make its way around the Festival in a matter of minutes. She was debating whether or not to follow after Thomas when someone grabbed her arm. She jumped around in surprise, her hand automatically going for her dagger.

"No need for that, young lady. Now what's this I hear about your running off with a boy? When I found Erinn and Lissa they couldn't stop talking about how you were so taken with him." Gregory stood in front of her with a dozen soldiers behind him.

"Father, you're not going to believe what I saw."

She quickly filled him in on her entire day, from going to the archery contest to spending time with Thomas. She kept her experience with magic to herself, just as Thomas had requested. Her father had a hard time keeping up with her excited explanation.

"Slow down, lass. Slow down." Gregory held his hands up in mock surrender. "You say this boy's name is Thomas? Are you sure he's the one?"

"Yes, Father, absolutely certain."

Gregory's expression turned thoughtful. "It's getting late, Kaylie. Let's head back to the castle."

As they made their way through the crowds, Kaylie went over her day in more detail, yet Gregory's mind was elsewhere. If this boy shot with the accuracy Kaylie spoke of, then he had little doubt that it was the same person who had helped them against the Fearhounds. Only a handful of people could shoot like that, if any. He would have to meet this Thomas. There were several questions he wanted to ask him. In particular, the name of his grandfather.

19

PLAN SET IN MOTION

"You have done well, Ragin. Better than I expected. Is this boy really the one we want?"

"I'd stake my life on it, Father." Ragin's face glowed with pride, thinking of how his sister would react to his latest coup. "His green eyes glowed when I saw him in the shadows of the forest. He has to be the one you had mentioned."

"You might have to," said Rodric harshly, turning to Lord Chertney, whose very presence chilled the room. The proximity of the man, who had arrived earlier in the day, seemingly out of nowhere, set him on edge. "Will my son's plan work?"

"Even a strong will can be manipulated, if you know how to do it properly," he replied. "I shall provide Ragin with exactly what he needs. Then we can determine if this boy is truly the one we want."

20

RENDEZVOUS

Kaylie examined herself in the mirror for the tenth time that morning, her expression thoughtful as she searched for flaws in her appearance. She had tried on more than a dozen riding dresses, finally selecting one in a dark purple that accentuated her eyes. Not that that was important, of course. She just felt like looking her best today. That was all, she confirmed to her image in the mirror once again.

Yet each time she said it, Kaylie found it harder and harder to believe. Still, she clung tenaciously to that belief. She refused to admit to herself that Thomas had affected her in some way. It just wouldn't be proper for a princess to fawn over a boy. All she wanted was another lesson in magic and nothing more.

Kaylie had thought about Thomas constantly since talking with him the day before, finding it almost impossible to get his flashing green eyes out of her mind, as well as the feeling she had experienced while learning more about this natural power. The remarkable incident with the bear had taken up most of the conversation the previous night, that and the archery contest, much to Ragin's chagrin. Everyone in the Palace was talking about it.

Unfortunately, her father would not allow her to go off on her own, and she certainly didn't want him to come along. He had shown far too much interest in Thomas, which made her distinctly uncomfortable. Every time this forest boy came up in conversation, a strange look came to her father's face, as if some long-lost memory had sprung free.

Biting her lip, she spun around a final time to make sure the dress fit her just the way she wanted. It would just have to do. Slipping her dagger into her belt, she stepped out into the large sitting room of their suite.

"My, my Father. You certainly do look dashing this morning."

Gregory colored slightly, not used to receiving compliments for his wardrobe. He normally wore grey or blue in simple cuts. Clothes did not make a king after all. Ability was the most important factor — at least in Fal Carrach. Because of that, the clothes he had chosen made him slightly uncomfortable. His deep blue trousers and clean white shirt were not that bad. But the red sash around his waist that matched his red and blue striped jacket seemed a bit much. Though his sword looked out of place, he had strapped it on out of habit.

"Are you sure I look all right?" he asked with worry. "This jacket just doesn't feel right."

"You look very debonair," Kaylie answered with a grin. "Almost swashbuckling." Her father blushed even more. It certainly was fun, and easy, to torture him.

Gregory immediately began pulling off the jacket.

"I was just kidding, father," she said, putting the jacket back over his shoulders. "You look very elegant."

And he did. This wasn't like him at all. He normally didn't care too much about his appearance, yet he had even combed his beard this morning.

"What's the occasion?"

"Sarelle wanted to discuss some trade agreements before going down to the Festival," he said sheepishly.

Kaylie chuckled softly. She doubted that the topic of trade would even come up. "Have fun, father. I'm off so see some of the vendors' wares at the festival." She walked quickly to the door.

"Hold on, young lady." The way she rushed out the door put Gregory instantly on alert. "Who are you going with?"

"No one. I feel like having some time to myself," she said innocently.

Gregory watched her for a few seconds. She was holding something back, but there was no sense in trying to get it out of her.

"And you will be back before dark?"

"Yes, Father." She knew he was going to ask that question. "I'll be back well before dark."

"All right," he said. "Just be careful. And watch out for Ragin. There's something about that boy that sets my teeth on edge."

"Don't worry, Father. He does the same to me. Have a good time with Sarelle."

Kaylie quickly stepped out into the hallway, glad that she had escaped her father so easily. If he hadn't been so distracted by the attentions of the Queen of Benewyn, he probably would have sent a troop of soldiers along with her.

Her suspicions about Sarelle's intent were instantly confirmed. The Queen of Benewyn stood just outside the door in a beautiful green dress. Her blazing red hair pulled into a bun surrounded by a modest circlet of silver looked magnificent. Obviously, trade agreements were the last thing on her mind.

"Ah, Kaylie. So good to see you."

"And a pleasure to see you, Queen Sarelle."

Was Sarelle nervous? Perhaps, but Kaylie couldn't tell for

sure. The Queen of Benewyn was always so confident — she had to be considering men ruled all the other Kingdom — yet Kaylie could pick up the distinct traces of a few minuscule breaches in her facade. She was absolutely certain that Sarelle had no intention of talking trade today.

"My father is just inside. He's anxiously awaiting you."

"Excellent," beamed Sarelle, her smile radiant.

"I hope you and father have a good time at the Festival," she said, walking down the hallway toward the stables.

"I'm sure we will," answered Sarelle. "I'm sure we will."

There was a mischievous gleam in her eye. Kaylie laughed softly as she turned the corner. She hoped her father knew what he was getting himself into. Once Sarelle had him tied around her finger, he'd never succeed in unraveling the string. Then again, perhaps he wouldn't want to.

21

THRILL OF SOMETHING NEW

Arriving at the clearing from the day before, Kaylie dropped the basket on the ground. She had visited the kitchens after getting past her father. The Dunmoorian cook had certainly been thorough, packing a wine cask, several different cheeses, some cold chicken and ham and a dozen different sweet tarts.

Coming to a stream, she followed its bank for a time, watching the water ripple across the rocks and branches beneath it. Maybe coming out here was a bad idea. Thomas had probably left for his home already, wherever that home may be. Off to the east somewhere. She had failed to pry anything more than that from him.

Feeling her irritation rise to the surface once more, she waded into the stream and stared down at the water. Remembering how she had connected with nature with Thomas the day before, she concentrated with all her might on the water flowing beneath her, trying to push her consciousness into it, to expand her senses and discover what lay beneath the surface. She remained where she was for several minutes, doing all she could, but nothing happened.

"You've almost got it," said a voice behind her, feeling a light touch on her hand. "Try this."

In a flash she was beneath the surface and coasting along the bottom of the stream. Excitement surged within her. She could hear the rush of the water and taste its sweetness. Instead of just swimming in it, she felt as if she were actually part of it. As if her essence had mixed with that of the stream and the two were inseparable. The fish and crayfish were a part of it, too, even the rocks and sand that formed the streambed. The power of nature was in everything around her, and as she raced through the water she could feel its pulse.

The entire experience contained a sense of awesome responsibility, but it also offered freedom — a freedom she had never felt before. Just as quickly as she had been beneath the waves, she was back on the streambed, her hand released. Yet she could still hear the constant beat of nature in her ears.

"What is it called?"

Kaylie asked in wonder. She kept her eyes closed, trying to ward off the encroaching dizziness from the rush of leaving the stream.

"The Talent," replied Thomas, stepping around Kaylie so he stood next to her. "It is the life force of nature. If it disappeared, then the world would end, for nature would be dead. Yesterday you worried that its source was Dark Magic. Actually, Dark Magic comes from the Talent, but in a perverted form. That story is neither here nor there, though. Did you enjoy the ride?"

"Yes, very much," replied Kaylie, turning to look at Thomas. His eyes twinkled with delight as he took in her cheeks flushed with excitement and broad grin. "The protector of animals and people returns."

Thomas blushed at Kaylie's pronouncement, scuffing his foot in the dirt, unsure of what to say. Kaylie found his discomfiture quite appealing.

"You almost had it, you know," said Thomas, trying to change the subject.

"What was I doing wrong? I tried to do exactly what you showed me yesterday, but I kept running into this wall that I couldn't pass through."

"That was the problem," said Thomas, who began walking along the stream with Kaylie following after him. "You kept trying to push your way through the wall. Next time, instead of banging your head against it time after time, stay relaxed and focused. Try a gentle but persistent nudge. If you do it right, the wall will crumble. It's all just a matter of concentration. Once you do it, once you break through the wall, you'll never have that problem again."

"That's very easy for you to say, you know," said Kaylie. "You can already do this."

"Maybe," said Thomas with a smile. "But I rarely get the opportunity to teach anyone something. Usually I'm the student."

Thomas leaped across the stream to the other side. Kaylie considered joining him, then decided against it. She had chosen her riding dress to impress him. Unfortunately she'd probably get tangled in all its folds if she tried jumping across. Falling face first into the stream was not what she had in mind. Instead she studied his face.

He was not as handsome as Ragin or Maddan, but there was something else there that she found even more attractive. A strength, perhaps, or a sense of purpose. Though his eyes flashed with merriment, there was always an underlying seriousness to them. Duty. Responsibility. She had never thought such qualities would appeal to her. She shook her head almost imperceptibly to clear her mind. What was she doing? Acting like Lissa or Erinn, or even worse, Jenna? She came here to learn from Thomas, not fawn all over him. He simply wasn't her type.

"How is the bear?"

Thomas smiled. "He's fine. He was cut in several places by the whip, but I cleaned out his wounds and applied some balms. He should be back in the Highlands by now. I told him to stay in the upper passes, so he won't have to worry about people like Falsuto."

Thomas spoke as if it was the most normal thing in the world to do — speak with animals. The whole thing astonished her. How could a human being talk to an animal? Yet that bear, ferocious and angry one minute, was as docile as a pet as soon as Thomas approached him. It was the most remarkable thing she had ever seen.

"You told him to stay in the upper passes?"

"Yes, I did," said Thomas, jumping back to her side of the stream. "Kaylie, just because someone says something is impossible, or it seems impossible, doesn't mean it is."

She liked the way Thomas said her name. She liked it a lot, though she tried not to admit it to herself.

"I'll try to remember that."

"Would you walk with me?" he asked, offering her his arm. His voice was confident, but his eyes uncertain.

"It would be my pleasure," she replied, taking his arm and steering him farther down the streambed.

They walked in silence for several minutes, simply enjoying one another's company.

"I assume that what happened yesterday got around the Festival quickly."

Kaylie laughed with pleasure. She was having more fun than she had had in a long time.

"You could say that. Within twenty minutes the story spread all the way to the Palace. You know, Thomas, you really have a particular knack for getting under people's skins."

"Oh, really? What do you mean by that?"

"Well, not only did you beat Ragin in the archery contest, but then you help win a bear's freedom? Everyone was talking about you, and Ragin doesn't like it when people are talking about someone other than himself."

"Yes, well, I could see how he might get upset." Thomas' sarcasm was as thick as molasses. "I'll have to apologize to him the next time I see him."

"Yes, you really should," said Kaylie with mock seriousness. They both laughed. "What's that on your arm?"

Kaylie ran her hand over his forearm. The wrist guard was twisted around, revealing what looked to be a mark of some sort, though she couldn't quite make it out. Thomas quickly adjusted the wrist guard, covering up the mark.

"Just a scar," he said. "I got it when I was very young."

Kaylie glanced at Thomas. Was he telling her everything? She didn't think so. Then again, he had been particularly nimble at avoiding her questions yesterday. Nevertheless, the mark tugged at the edge of her memory. As she tried to remember where she had seen it before, the image of the raptor soaring above the plain appeared in her mind. The scar resembled the claw of the raptor. She'd have to get a better look at it to confirm her suspicions. Now why would something like this stick in her mind?

Thomas' heart leapt into his throat for a moment. Thankfully, he didn't think she had recognized the mark. He attempted to change the subject.

"So how long will you be in Tinnakilly?"

"For a few more days," said Kaylie. "To be honest, I can't wait to get home. I thought it would be fun to go to the Festival, but I'm growing tired of it — and particularly the company."

"You mean you're not having fun with your friends?"

Kaylie snorted. "My friends — Lissa, Jenna, and Erinn — are only interested in looking at boys, and Maddan in impressing me, yet he's not very good at it. In fact, it's almost embarrassing to watch him sometimes."

"And Ragin?" Thomas was curious about her relationship with the High King's son. Ragin had acted as if they were very close, yet Kaylie tried to keep her distance from him.

"Ragin is not my friend." She almost shouted it, then thought better of it. "He's a manipulative jackass."

"I'm sorry. I didn't mean to upset you."

Thomas had not expected such a harsh response. Still, it pleased him.

"It's not your fault. So when are you going home? You told me it was to the east, but you never said exactly where."

Thomas smiled. She was tenacious, wasn't she? He had a feeling that when she wanted something she got it, if only from sheer willpower, which meant she probably wasn't used to his vague responses.

"I was going to leave today, but Beluil ran off somewhere, and I've got to wait for him. I'll probably go later today or tomorrow."

Kaylie looked at Thomas with annoyance. He was such a guarded person, having dodged her question again. Well, he could play his game as long as he wanted. She'd get answers to her questions eventually. It was just a matter of time.

"Do you mind if I ask you a more personal question?"

"Not at all," said Thomas. His stomach filled with butterflies. He wondered what she was after this time.

"Can you speak with any animal you want?"

Thomas relaxed. "Pretty much. It's usually a question of whether or not the animal wants to speak with me."

"Then how do you do it?"

Thomas appeared slightly embarrassed. "To be honest, I don't really know. It's just something I do. I think it has something to do with the Talent. Much like I can actually become a part of nature, I can use the same power to speak with animals,

I just have to manipulate it in a slightly different way. I'm sorry, but that's the best explanation I can offer."

Kaylie stopped and faced Thomas, her expression one of annoyance. "You know, Thomas, you can be an extremely frustrating person."

"I know," he replied with a mischievous grin. "I've been told that several times before, most often by a very beautiful woman."

"Oh, really," said Kaylie, placing her hands on her hips and tapping one foot. Her interest was suddenly heightened, and Thomas sensed some jealousy. She resembled a lioness preparing to strike. "And just who might this beautiful woman be?"

Thomas laughed. Rya would be pleased to know that she could still fluster another woman.

"Are you jealous, Kaylie?"

"I most certainly am not," she replied a little too vehemently, hitting him lightly in the chest.

Her words said one thing but her bright red face said another. Why would she be jealous? She barely even knew Thomas.

"I didn't think so," said Thomas, grinning from ear to ear. It certainly was fun teasing her.

"Good," replied Kaylie, smoothing the folds of her riding dress.

Why had she reacted that way? She had known Thomas for two days and already she was acting like a jealous lover. What had gotten into her?

"You're the Princess of Fal Carrach after all. It just wouldn't be proper, now would it?"

"It most certainly would not," replied Kaylie.

She adopted the tone she used when giving orders, but one glance at Thomas' grin told her he was egging her on. She immediately hit him in the chest again, this time a little harder.

His small grunt of pain gave her a certain satisfaction, and she smiled herself.

"As I said, Thomas, you are an extremely difficult person." And mysterious, and exciting, and interesting, but she'd keep that to herself.

22

TAKEN BY SURPRISE

"Why don't we have a look at what's in the picnic basket? I'm famished."

"Sounds good," replied Kaylie, grasping his hand.

She thought to only lead him back to the clearing, but once she felt the warmth of his touch, she was reluctant to let go.

As they entered the glade, Thomas spread out the blanket, placing the bow and sword he carried beside him, as Kaylie began pulling items out of the basket.

"It looks wonderful," he said. "Did you do this yourself?"

"Of course I did," she lied, her grin giving her away.

Kaylie had never cooked before. She had never seen the need as someone always did it for her. Settling down on the blanket, she crossed her legs and began passing plates of food over to Thomas.

They sat in silence for a few moments, as both took a few bites of food. Several minutes passed before Thomas was ready to talk.

"Are you all right, Kaylie? You seem pensive."

Kaylie jumped at the mention of her name, realizing she had drifted off into her own little world. She could get used to this, she thought. The peace, the quiet, the privacy. She looked up from her food and saw a faraway look on Thomas' face.

"What were you doing, Thomas?"

"Just checking to see what's around," replied Thomas.

"You mean checking for any danger?"

The thought excited her, which made Kaylie worried. The time she had spent with Thomas differed greatly from her life in the Rock, and she was beginning to enjoy it a bit too much, she thought, if the possibility of danger pleased her.

"I guess you could say that," he said, biting into a piece of bread thick with butter.

"And did you find anything?"

"Nothing to worry about," he replied.

"So where's Beluil today?" she asked, surprised at the disappointment she felt at his announcement.

"He's exploring the forest, looking for other wolves most likely."

"Do you spend all of your time wandering in the forest, Thomas, or do you actually have a home?"

"I have a home," he replied, settling back on the blanket and eating some goat cheese. It was quite good actually. "I try to stay away from it as much as possible, though."

"You don't like it there?"

"No, I do. I don't mean to give you the wrong impression. I like my home very much. It's just that my grandparents are firm believers in the dictum that idle hands lead to mischief. Whenever I'm home they always find work for me to do, most of it boring, so I try to stay away. It's more fun wandering in the forest, as you call it."

"I know what you mean," replied Kaylie. "My father is much the same way. If he sees me with nothing to do, he's always willing to make use of my time. Very gracious of him, don't you think?" The sarcasm dripped from her voice.

Thomas chuckled softly. "I have a feeling that your father

and my grandparents would get along just fine." Thomas leaned forward for a slice of bread, Kaylie's eyes tracing his movements carefully, taking in everything about him. "Of course, even when I'm there, they're not always satisfied with my work."

"You get into trouble regularly, don't you?" Kaylie guessed. Her smile made Thomas' heart beat faster.

"Yes, I do. How did you know?"

"Your eyes," she said. "They're full of mischief."

"Maybe that's what gives me away all the time. I can never seem to get away with anything when my grandparents are around. It's like they have eyes on the backs of their heads. In fact my grandmother got so angry with me once, she threatened to kick me off the island."

An island? Thomas lived on an island. Either Thomas' defenses had slipped or he was beginning to feel more comfortable talking with her. That possibility thrilled her, yet also sent a shiver of fear through her body. Why was she suddenly afraid?

"And just how did that happen?"

Thomas glanced at Kaylie, noting her interest. He normally wasn't one to tell stories — that was his grandfather's specialty — but he decided to give it a try anyway.

"Well, one time my grandmother wanted to expand the garden behind our cottage, so she told me to clear the rocks from the field. Now, where we live, the soil is filled with rocks, some almost as large as this." Thomas extended his arms to their full length. "It wasn't an easy task. And unfortunately I couldn't find a way out of it. I started that morning, not even stopping for lunch, and was going to finish in the afternoon. But Beluil came by and convinced me to do some exploring with him."

"Beluil convinced you?" Kaylie asked skeptically, thinking the wolf couldn't be the principal culprit.

"A wolf can be very persuasive, you know." Kaylie's expression said that she didn't, but Thomas continued the story anyway. "I had cleared nearly half the field and thought I could finish the following day. My grandmother had something else in mind, however, as she wasn't very pleased with me not finishing the job."

Thomas leaned forward and scrunched up his face, his voice coming out as a screech. "'I want this field cleared by tomorrow,' she told me. 'I don't care if you have to work through the night.'"

Thomas leaned back, smiling as he remembered the incident, though at the time he was anything but pleased.

"When I protested, she said it would help build my character."

Thomas' expression said he clearly didn't believe a word of it. Kaylie laughed at his imitation, wondering if his grandmother was really as bad as Thomas made her out to be.

"As you can imagine, I wasn't very happy about that at all. She'd been telling me for years that my chores would build character, but I could never figure out why that would be and had seen no evidence of it. Now, my grandmother isn't the type of person you can simply disregard. So I kept at it and finished just before dawn."

Thomas' voice lowered, as if he were about to tell Kaylie a secret. "My grandmother is an early riser and she got up soon after I was done. She immediately wanted to see my handiwork and tried to get out of the cottage. But she couldn't. I'd piled a whole bunch of rocks against the door just to get back at her for making me work through the night."

Kaylie laughed at the image that appeared in her mind. She could see the grin on Thomas' face as he watched her grandmother struggle with the door to her home, not knowing why it wouldn't open.

"As I said, you're trouble."

"Maybe so," he replied. "My fun was short-lived, though. After I removed the rocks from the door — now keep in mind it was just a prank — my grandmother was, well, irritated."

"Just irritated?" asked Kaylie, trying to keep a straight face.

"Furious was more like it," replied Thomas. "She took one look at me, her face red with anger, and then examined the field. I expected her to start yelling, but instead she turned to me with her own smile and said, 'I've changed my mind. Put the rocks back where you found them. I like it better with the rocks.' As you can guess, I was not happy. As a result I no longer play any pranks on my grandmother. It's not worth the risk."

Kaylie couldn't stop laughing, imagining the scene as it played out before her. Finally, she caught her breath.

"And did you put all the rocks back?"

"Thankfully my grandfather convinced my grandmother to leave everything as it was. You know, he still holds that over my head to this very day. He keeps telling me that sometime soon I'll have to pay him back for the favor he did me."

"It sounds like you have quite an interesting family, Thomas."

Kaylie enjoyed listening to him. It was refreshing to talk with someone whose ego wasn't as large as a peak in the Highlands or who didn't spend all of his time bragging.

"Interesting is an understatement," he replied in a short laugh. "Sometimes you just can't win."

"I know what you mean," she said. "When my mother died my father was devastated. He really did his best raising me, but it was tough on him. Sometimes he didn't know what to do with me."

At the mention of her mother a black cloud appeared over Thomas, anger and grief apparent in his features. It quickly disappeared. Did he lose his mother as well? Or was it the mention of her father?

"When my father was busy, Kael or some of the other

soldiers would look after me, which is probably why I'm not interested in things like knitting or singing or the other stuff you're supposed to learn as a lady of the court. My father is extremely protective. When he saw me riding a horse for the first time — I must have been five or six — he almost had a fit. Kael had taken me down to the stables for the morning and found a small pony for me."

Kaylie's face brightened as she recalled the experience, setting Thomas' heart racing.

"We were in a small compound and Kael was leading me around. The pony must have been twenty years old, so the only thing it wanted to do was walk, and slowly at that. When my father came out his face turned completely red and it looked like he was foaming at the mouth." She laughed as she remembered the image. "He was so upset he threatened to throw Kael in the dungeon."

"He didn't, though, did he?"

The name Kael Bellilil had stuck with him since the previous night. Oso had mentioned it to him once. From what he remembered, Kael was a Highlander who did what he thought best, without regard for the consequences. Hence, his decision to leave the Highlands for Fal Carrach. Going amicably to the dungeons didn't sound like him at all.

"No, he didn't. Kael has always been good with my father. They've known each other for such a long time, my father listens to Kael's advice before anyone else's. Kael convinced him that there was no need to worry. Still, ever since then I've been more a tomboy than a princess, much to my father's aggravation."

"There's nothing wrong with that."

"No, there isn't, except when you're supposed to be a queen someday. It wasn't until we ran into you in the Burren that he actually let me learn swordplay."

"Glad to be of service," replied Thomas as he finished off a piece of cheese. The tangy flavor appealed to him.

"If I was a boy, you know, I would never have had any trouble at all. Because I'm a girl everyone has always thought that I couldn't do this or I shouldn't do that. It's all extremely frustrating."

"I can imagine. It's strange, though."

"What do you mean?" she asked.

"I don't see why being a girl, or woman, should prevent you from doing something, whether it's learning how to ride a horse or handle a blade or anything else for that matter."

"My thinking exactly," grinned Kaylie, pleased by his words. "Being a princess certainly isn't all it's made out to be."

"And what if you weren't a princess?" asked Thomas. "What would you do then?"

The question surprised Kaylie. No one had ever asked her that before. She had never even considered it herself.

"What would I do? I don't know."

Thomas smiled at her, wiping his hands free of crumbs. "Well, whatever you chose, I'm sure it would be quite interesting."

"Why do you say that?"

Thomas looked at her as if he were slightly embarrassed. "I don't know," he replied. "Although I haven't known you for very long, it's clear that you're the type of person who follows her heart. You're willing to take a chance and do what you think is right regardless of what others think. That's all."

Kaylie stared at Thomas in shock. He knew her better than she knew herself. The beating of her heart drowned out everything around her for a brief moment and it took her a few seconds to regain her composure.

Looking down at the blanket a bit embarrassed, she noticed she had forgotten to serve something.

"Would you like some wine?"

Thomas was unlike anyone else she knew. Quiet, honest, not trying to impress her. He was confident in himself, but not arrogant. And shy, too. It was perhaps the last quality that made her heart beat even faster.

"I've never drunk wine before."

"Then you should try it," she decided. "Just to see what it tastes like." She poured him a glass and handed it to him.

Unable to say no to her, Thomas took a few swallows and put the glass down. He didn't like the sweet flavor, and it tasted almost gritty. Having never drunk wine before, perhaps that was simply the way it was supposed to taste. If that was the case, he had certainly not missed anything by abstaining.

"It's really not to my liking."

"Do you mind if I ask you a personal question, Thomas?"

He nodded. "Go ahead."

"What's the most important quality you look for in a person? You know, in terms of a friend."

Thomas sat there a moment, considering how to respond. He wasn't feeling very well all of a sudden. Looking up at Kaylie, her features appeared fuzzy. He tried rubbing his eyes to clear them. This was strange. Very strange. A few small swallows of wine shouldn't have had such an effect on him. It took several seconds for him to answer her question.

"Trust. It would have to be trust. I would have to be able to trust the person before I could call him or her a friend."

23

———————

BETRAYAL

"Do you think you could learn to trust me, Thomas?" Her heart was in her throat as she asked the question, unsure if she could handle a negative reply.

"I already do, Kaylie. I already do." Thomas sat up and began rubbing his forehead, trying to clear his head.

"Are you all right, Thomas?" He seemed to be a bit green.

"Something doesn't feel right," he said, his words coming out slurred.

Thomas shook his head in an effort to clear the darkness sweeping over him. He stood up slowly, sword in hand, and almost fell back down. His legs were unsteady and his eyes refused to focus. Men approached. Men with a foul taint. He could feel them coming closer, but his senses were dulled. He had made a mistake, perhaps even a fatal mistake.

The soldiers walked into the clearing from all sides. Thomas spun around and almost lost his balance in the process. He struggled just to remain on his feet. He understood now what had happened to him, something he had been a fool not to consider. He glanced down at Kaylie, seeing the soldiers for the first time.

"I trusted you," he whispered.

Kaylie saw the betrayal in his eyes, the pain. "But Thomas, I had nothing to do with this. I swear—"

"Drop your sword, Thomas. You can't escape."

Thomas recognized the voice. The figures circling the glade flitted around like shadows. The only thing he could see clearly was their drawn swords. Still, he would never forget that voice. Ragin Tessaril. He was a fool. His grandfather had always said to expect almost anything. Once again he had ignored common sense. A princess who actually wanted to see him again? Why would a princess be interested in him? He scoffed at the thought now. No, there was always some underlying agenda. He should have known. And this time he had figured it out too late.

"Drop your sword, Thomas!"

The voice came from his left this time. Thomas turned in that direction. The blackness in his mind threatened to overwhelm him. It took all of his strength to fight it off.

"I think not."

"The High King is looking forward to meeting you, Thomas," said Ragin, pulling his own sword from its scabbard. "He never said in what condition you were to be brought to him, though. Take him."

Instead of waiting for the soldiers to come to him, Thomas stumbled forward, making for where he had heard the sound of steel escaping from its sheath. His action surprised the soldiers, but no one more so than Ragin. Unprepared to defend himself, Ragin jumped backwards and yanked a soldier in front of him. Thomas' blade connected in the space between the man's neck and breastplate, killing him instantly.

With Ragin out of reach, Thomas turned to meet the onrushing soldiers. He considered running into the forest, but was certain that in his current condition he wouldn't make it very far. Normally he would be able to blend into the foliage, but the drug now in his system made his motions clumsy and clouded his mind. As a result, he could barely stand up. A strong breeze could knock him on his back and he'd be as defenseless as a turtle. He tried to concentrate, to take hold of the Talent, but it slipped through his fingers and out of his grasp. He swore in frustration. He couldn't focus on anything but the blackness, which slowly consumed his consciousness.

Fighting more by instinct than sight, Thomas met the charge of two soldiers, catching both their blades on his own. He kicked out with one leg and almost lost his balance, but thankfully his foot connected with the soldier's jaw. The man fell backward, allowing Thomas to focus on the other soldier. Pushing him back, Thomas lunged forward. The soldier dodged out of the way, but he did not expect the quick slash as Thomas stepped back that caught him in the neck. The man fell to the ground, his life bleeding out onto the thick grass of the clearing.

Thomas spun, bringing his blade around in a wide arc and catching the soldier charging behind him at the waist. The blade bit deeply, the man falling down in anguish as his innards spilled out of the gaping wound. Two more soldiers ran toward him. Unsure of their exact location, Thomas swung wildly with his blade. His luck held, as the blade met one soldier's unprotected head. The other soldier, shocked by the quick death of his comrade, looked down at his friend in amazement. He never felt Thomas' blade as it slipped through his stomach.

Stumbling forward, Thomas tried to defend himself. He couldn't remember how many soldiers he had killed, or how many remained. The number of attackers finally caught up with him, though, as the drug in his system worked its way through his body. Swinging at another attacker, the motion put him off balance, and he fell to his knees. He never had the opportunity to get back up as three soldiers jumped on him, one knocking his sword from his hand while the other two pushed him down into the grass.

Several more soldiers piled on. When they realized their quarry was finally defeated, they kicked at him blindly with their steel-tipped boots, catching Thomas in the stomach, the back, his legs, his face. He grunted with each kick that connected, thankful that the drug dulled his senses and took the sting from the attack. The blackness eventually took him, Thomas drifted off into a dreamless sleep.

"Stop it!" yelled Kaylie, surging to her feet and running to the group of soldiers surrounding Thomas, tears streaming down her cheeks. "Stop it, damn you. Stop it!"

She tried pulling the soldiers away but they shrugged off her efforts, continuing to kick Thomas until Ragin intervened.

"Enough. My father wanted him alive."

Ragin put his sword back in its scabbard and walked across the clearing. The soldiers stepped aside so he could take a closer look at their captive. Bruises and cuts covered Thomas' face, and his stomach and back probably looked much the same. Still, it didn't appear that his men had broken any bones. His father would be quite pleased.

"You didn't mix enough willowbark with the wine, Lesti."

"I did, my prince. Truly I did." A soldier of average height stepped forward, still breathing heavily from doing his part to subdue Thomas. "It usually only takes a pinch, my prince. If I put in any more a normal man would have died. Willowbark is an excellent sleeping agent, but if too much is ingested it becomes a poison."

Ragin grunted. Nothing ever seemed to be easy with this forest whelp.

Kaylie stared down at Thomas during Ragin's examination, wiping the tears from her eyes. What had she done to him?

"The boy will hang, Kaylie," said Ragin, sneering across Thomas' still form. "He murdered five of my men."

"He defended himself!" she screamed, finding it difficult to control her emotions. Her hand went to her dagger, and she considered pulling it free, but to what use? There were too many soldiers surrounding her.

"From what?" Ragin stood up.

"From your men, you bastard!"

Kaylie's reserve was slowly breaking apart. Thomas had been attacked, but she suddenly realized that she was the only person there who would attest to that. Once they returned to Tinnakilly, Thomas was a dead man.

"Why would he try to escape?" asked Ragin in a soothing voice.

"Because he knew what would happen if he was taken!"

"You won't understand, Kaylie. You never will." Ragin shook his head, disappointment clear in his face. "Besides, it was because of you that he was captured. Why should you even bother to defend him now? The evidence is clear. And when he awakens he'll certainly hate you more than he will me. And by the look in his eyes when he charged, he hates me quite a lot."

Ragin walked toward his horse, which one of his soldiers had brought forward.

"Throw him onto the back of one of the horses, and don't be too gentle about it." Several men ran forward eager to obey. "Thank you, Kaylie. You have done us a great service."

Kaylie ignored him, watching as the soldiers threw Thomas' limp body onto a horse, tying his arms and legs to the saddle. *Why did you do this? Why?* She didn't know how to reply. The questions finally stopped, only to be replaced by something worse. She could hear Thomas' voice now, repeating the simple words over and over. Each time they cut into her just a little more until she felt raw on the inside. *I trusted you. I trusted you.* He had trusted her, and in return she had betrayed him.

24

FORESHADOWING

As the soldiers threw Thomas onto the horse, a Raptor watched from above, slowly circling the clearing, its search for prey momentarily forgotten. The large predator sensed that something evil had occurred, shifting the balance nature shared with the shadow. A dark time was coming, spurred on by what had happened below. Still, it could only watch, and wait. One of its own had been taken. One that was meant to be free. One that was meant to stand tall against the onrushing darkness.

25

LOOKING FOR HELP

Beluil ran through the forest in the rapidly fading light. Night was almost upon the land, the sun fading. He was still musing about the grey and white she-wolf he had spent the last few days with. He wanted to tell Thomas about her. She really was quite attractive, at least to a wolf. Thomas would understand. He always did.

Beluil broke through the foliage and ran into the clearing that had served as their campsite for the last week. He expected to see Thomas here already, waiting impatiently, but the glade was empty. His friend's pack remained hidden behind the tree and the grass showed no sign of footsteps.

Though the clearing looked as if no one had ever stopped there before, Beluil knew better. Thomas was very meticulous, taking the time to bring the grass back to life where they had slept on it the night before so if anyone happened by, nothing would appear out of place. Yet to him, on this cool evening, something about the clearing felt wrong. The wolf stood there for a moment, sniffing the wind. His yellow eyes glowed brightly in the dusk and were his only visible feature as his black fur blended into the deepening darkness. Thomas should have returned by now. Yet there was no sign of him.

Beluil ran in the direction Thomas had left that morning, picking up his scent almost immediately, though it was very faint. Too much time had passed since Thomas had last come this way. He would not have been able to follow it if he had not known it so well. The hours passed as Beluil steadily grew closer to Tinnakilly, finally entering a small clearing with a stream running through it.

Jumping over the flowing water, he stopped in the middle of the glade. A blanket lay in its center, one corner flapping in the wind. A basket full of food and a wine bottle held it down. As Beluil scanned the glade with his eyes, the signs of a struggle became apparent.

The scent of his friend was strong here, as well as the scents of many others. Dark scents. He quickly made a circuit of the camp, noting the blood staining the grass in a half-dozen places. A flash of steel caught his eye, hidden partly beneath the blanket. Thomas' sword. Beluil growled in anger. Something was wrong. Terribly wrong.

Beluil took a final look around to make sure he hadn't missed anything, then ran to the west at an easy pace through the woods and out onto the grassland. The scent was strong here, and the large wolf increased his pace. As he followed the trail, a misty rain began to fall, increasing in intensity as the minutes passed.

The wolf was soaked to the bone, but still he pressed on, knowing that time was of the essence. The rain was washing out the trail and he was losing the scent. Finally, as the steady rain became a downpour, the scent disappeared completely. Beluil had almost reached the river, and across its expanse he saw the faint lights of a city.

He howled in frustration, the cry of anguish drifting for miles across the open space. He could do nothing for his friend now, for his brother. But he would not fail him. Thomas was west of the river, that much he knew. He would return to the Isle of Mist and Rynlin and Rya would help him. But first he would retrieve Thomas' sword. Trying to communicate with Thomas' grandparents was difficult, as they did not have Thomas' abilities. The sword would tell them what they needed to know.

26

———————

SUCCESS

K aylie's trip back to Tinnakilly passed in a blur, every mile a waking nightmare. She rode behind the horse carrying Thomas, unable to take her eyes from him. All the while she could hear his voice in her head: *I trusted you. I trusted you.*

A driving rain began as they passed under the portcullis of the castle. She didn't bother putting on the hooded cloak one of the soldiers passed to her. Though she was soaked to the bone, her hair plastered to her head and her clothes drenched, she was numb to everything around her, even the cold rain.

As Ragin led his squadron of soldiers through the Palace gates, Kaylie thought only of the terrible mistake she had made. The world around her no longer mattered. She almost welcomed the hard rainfall, imagining the drops pelted the ground in anger at the capture of one of their own, the hard wind howling its displeasure, the thunder and lightning echoing their rage. Thomas should be free, but he wasn't — because of her.

The courtyard of the keep was deserted because of the storm, except for one person who waited there, his grin matching that of his son's. Rodric Tessaril clapped his hands in pleasure when he saw the bundle strapped to one of the horses. The four other riderless horses didn't even register with him. His plan had succeeded. That was all that mattered. Ragin rode straight to his father, who grabbed the bridle as his son jumped into the mud.

"You've done well, Ragin. I'm impressed."

"Thank you, father."

Ragin's normal boastfulness failed him at that moment, taken aback by his father's compliment. His father normally offered screams of anger and shouts of rage, not kind words.

Rodric dropped the horse's bridle in his son's hand and walked over to the horse carrying Thomas. His grin grew bigger, displaying his rather unwieldy teeth. Taking hold of Thomas' hair, he looked into the unconscious face of his nemesis. His master would be pleased, but first Rodric would have his fun. This whelp had been a thorn in his foot for much too long.

"Enjoy it while you can, boy. Your head won't be attached to your shoulders much longer." Rodric laughed softly as his pleasure momentarily defeated his normal recalcitrance. "Put him in the dungeon. I'll be down to check on him later."

Four soldiers jumped from their horses and began the process of unstrapping Thomas. After unceremoniously dumping him into the mud, they each picked up an arm or a leg and carried the unconscious boy into the Palace.

Kaylie remained on her horse, unable to fathom the true extent of what she had unwittingly done until Rodric's words jolted her from her stupor. Rodric had used her. She could barely stand the thought that she was responsible for his capture. If she was responsible for his murder as well, she'd never be able to live with herself. Leaping down from her horse, she ran right up to Rodric.

"You're a monster!" she shouted, not caring who heard. "He

was defending himself. You have no right to do this to him. No right!"

She was so furious she could barely get the words out. Ragin had stepped behind his father, not wanting to get in the way of her tirade. Kaylie had found the target for her anger — for being used, for acting like a fool, for hurting someone who had just tried to be her friend — and she let it out full blast. Hurting someone who saw her as a person rather than a princess. Someone who didn't deserve to die at the hands of such a loathsome creature. High King he might be in name, but he certainly didn't deserve her respect.

"You're nothing but a murderer!"

"Are you finished, girl," interrupted Rodric, his face red with fury yet his voice soft and sibilant. He resembled a snake preparing to strike. Kaylie suddenly realized that she had stepped on very dangerous terrain. "You've done well, child. Better than I expected, in fact. Thank you for leading us to him."

"Why, blast it? I want to know why!" Tears formed in her eyes, though Rodric couldn't tell. The rain had increased in intensity, the heavy drops pounding into the muddy courtyard.

Rodric's eyes narrowed and this time Kaylie stepped back a pace. She was alone in the courtyard with Rodric and his soldiers. Kaylie had unknowingly placed herself in a potentially deadly situation.

"You may be the princess of Fal Carrach, girl, but I'm the High King." Rodric's sharp whisper carried through the rain and howling wind, and for the first time that day Kaylie shivered. "Even your father cannot protect you from me. I suggest you quiet your voice and be satisfied that I don't make an example of you here and now. You will learn that as you gain more power, you often have to use people to do what is necessary. Consider this your first, and only, lesson."

Rodric then turned on his heel with Ragin, smug expression in place, in tow. The scene at an end, the soldiers led their horses to the stables. As the courtyard cleared Kaylie dropped to the ground, not caring about the mud or pools of water. For the first time the full import of what she had done hit her. Unwittingly, she had sentenced a true friend to death.

27

SMUG SATISFACTION

As the rain pelted the Palace, Chertney watched the argument in the courtyard with great interest from under a small portico that protected him from the elements, yet gave him a full view of the drama as it played out. The princess had spirit, but was clearly inexperienced. To challenge Rodric at such a time was an obvious mistake. She was lucky, princess or no, that she'd be able to walk away. Next time, well, Rodric was not one to allow a next time for such things.

When Ragin had laid out his plan the night before, Chertney had never expected it would actually work. Ragin lacked any real strategic ability. And having that pompous whelp lead the expedition was a second mistake, but then again, the only person who really could ensure the mission's success was Kaylie, or to be even more accurate, himself.

If not for him and his use of Dark Magic to mask the attack, the boy would still be free, escaping before the soldiers arrived despite the drugged wine. He wallowed in his own vanity when the four soldiers carried their quarry past him on their way to the dungeon. Chertney was rudely knocked back to reality.

It couldn't be! It just wasn't possible! But it was! The resemblance was unmistakable. He had thought for years that talk of a green-eyed boy would simply result in the discovery of another — a boy similar to the one he had originally hunted so many years before in the Highlands. A boy he had thought long dead. But his master had been right. The boy had survived, and a dangerous man he had become.

For a brief moment Chertney wondered what had happened to the Nightstalker assigned to the boy, but then his question was answered for him. As the soldiers carried Thomas into the Palace, one of them tripped on a step, dropping the boy's shoulder to the stone as a result. The jolt knocked something out from underneath his shirt. A necklace. A necklace that Chertney recognized. The boy had become even more dangerous than he had ever thought possible, more dangerous than even his master believed.

"You see, Chertney, the plan was a success. Now what do you have to say to that?"

Rodric stood before him, having caught him by surprise as he considered this strange turn of events. He quickly regained his composure.

"You have done better than I expected, Rodric. You are to be commended."

Rodric chafed at the mocking tone adopted by Chertney, one normally reserved for a dog. The man was a fool, yet even fools got lucky, Chertney reminded himself. This fool probably didn't realize the true value of the prize he had just captured.

"You will do what is required?" he asked the gloating High King, once again wishing for the freedom to carve the smile from his ugly face.

"In time, Chertney. In time." Rodric was clearly pleased with himself and he was not yet ready to relinquish the feeling.

"Rodric, you know what our master requires. To delay could be—"

Rodric laughed off Chertney's worry. "Chertney, your concern surprises me. You sound like an old grandmother."

Chertney's normally pale face turned slightly red with anger. He did not enjoy being made the butt of jokes.

"Rodric, do not toy with me. Our master is not as understanding as I am."

Rodric immediately turned serious. "I am not a fool, Chertney, no matter what you might think. The task will be done, but it will be done my way. I am the High King, and an example must be made."

"As you say, Rodric," agreed Chertney. For the thousandth time the black-clad warlock cursed his predicament. Rodric was a worm and deserved to be crushed. No one had ever dared to speak to him, Lord Chertney, in such a way before. Yet he could not retaliate. Not yet, anyway. "As you say."

Nodding in satisfaction, Rodric strode into the Palace with his son following along behind him. Chertney watched them until the doors closed. Soon he was the only one left in the courtyard, watching the rain strike the ground for several minutes, deep in thought, oblivious to his surroundings.

This had certainly been an interesting turn of events. The question now was how he could profit by it. His master wanted the boy dead, and that could be easily accomplished. Then again, what would his master give if the boy appeared in Shadow's Reach alive? Perhaps the boy could be put to use in his master's cause. Then what reward would Chertney receive? Even greater power, or an immediate and painful death for disobeying his master's original command?

He didn't know. It would all depend on his master's mood. Still, to bring the boy to Shadow's Reach might be worth the risk. True, to spirit him away from Rodric could create problems with his master's alliance to Armagh, but then again, alliances were made to be broken. It was only a matter of time and circumstance. He would have to think carefully on it.

He could, of course, do nothing. And then, after Rodric had killed the boy, bring the news to his master, making it clear as to whom was really to thank for a job well done. That was the safest course of action, and many times the cautious approach was the wisest. Then again, sometimes a cautious approach was the same as a failed one. You just never knew until events finally came to a head.

Chertney would think more on it, but first there was something he must do. The Sylvana still existed, the boy's necklace having confirmed that unpleasant fact. Though he had never expected to hear of that fabled group again, they were now certainly a threat and definitely would come looking for the boy. He would protect against that. Then he would decide what to do. The more he thought about it, the more he realized he could not lose regardless of the action taken. The real question was how much could he win?

28

COMPETITORS

Ragin walked down the center of the hallway, forcing everyone else to move to the side. The angry looks his back received didn't bother him as they normally would. Usually, the tiniest slight, whether real or imagined, angered him. On this day, though, his grin ran from ear to ear. He had succeeded. Even better, he had never seen his father so pleased before, which made Ragin smile even more.

He was so caught up in his victory as he ventured toward his apartments that he almost knocked down a young woman who refused to get out of his way. Ragin bit back an oath and stared down at the diminutive blonde who stood calmly before him.

"Sister," he said coolly.

"Brother," replied Corelia, her eyes flashing, a seductive smile never far from her lips.

Though only a few years apart, they had never been very close. Each one saw the other as the primary rival for their father's power, and in fact it was a contest that their father encouraged. He constantly said that anyone could survive a battlefield of arms with luck, but only the strong could maneuver through the backstabbing and lies of politics. They had both taken that lesson to heart.

Unfortunately for Ragin, he had discovered at a very young age that matching wits with his sister was a losing proposition. So he had looked for other ways to get the better of her, as he had just accomplished with Thomas' capture.

"Have you heard?"

"Heard what?" she asked sharply. Beautiful and cunning she may be, but patient she was not.

"That I captured the Raptor earlier today. Kaylie led me right to him, and I personally took him into custody. As you can imagine, father is quite pleased." Ragin stood there regally, chest sticking out, puffed up by his perceived greatness.

Corelia studied her brother with a sly grin. "You mean the boy who defeated you in the archery competition? You don't even know if he is the Raptor."

She knew exactly how to get under her brother's skin, and this barb certainly did the trick, quickly deflating his ego and putting him in a sour mood. He did not like to be reminded of his failures, yet Corelia was all too happy to do so.

"He got lucky, that was all," he protested. "Besides, by tomorrow he'll be on the headsman's block, his victory just a dim memory."

"So what does Thomas look like?" she asked. "Tall? Handsome? Is he a friend of Kaylie's or just an acquaintance? Can he really talk with animals? Is he any good with a sword?"

Corelia's barrage of questions overwhelmed Ragin, each one darkening his mood even more. This was his time to celebrate, and once again his sister had spoiled it for him.

"Enough!" he shouted. "If you want answers to your questions, go ask someone else. I have better things to do."

"Sorry, Ragin. I didn't mean to upset you. I was just curious." Her tone said that she was anything but sorry. She stepped past her brother. "You've done well, Ragin. I'm glad to see that one of your plans finally worked out."

"Just what do you mean by that?" he exclaimed.

"You know exactly what I mean, brother dear," she laughed. "You better be careful, Ragin. If the stories are true about this boy" — and her voice implied that she hoped they were true — "you're playing with something even more dangerous than fire. Getting burned could be your most appealing alternative."

Corelia headed back down the hallway, not bothering to wait for her brother's response. It was another one of her tactics designed to irritate him, one that had worked quite well for years.

Ragin watched her go, his anger building. She'd get hers someday. He'd make sure about that. He quickly walked down the hallway to his apartments. He needed an outlet for his rage. Maybe he could find a serving girl. Yes, that was the perfect solution. And if she refused, all the better. His face twisted into a wicked grin as he went in search of his next victim.

29

A TRAP

Gregory sat comfortably in the cushioned chair just a few feet away from the blazing fire. The driving rainstorm and howling wind had sent a chill through the Palace. The warmth from the fireplace kept it at bay. That and the beautiful woman sitting across from him.

"As you well know, Gregory," said Sarelle Makarin, Queen of Benewyn, her green eyes glowing brightly thanks to the fire, "we are a kingdom of trade. We don't have time for people like Loris who think they can get whatever they want with an army."

Gregory listened to Sarelle half-heartedly, nodding his head at the appropriate times, as his mind wandered all too frequently. She truly was a beautiful woman. Gregory certainly appreciated that fact, but it was her other qualities that appealed to him more. Her intelligence and strength of character to name just a few. Those qualities were absolutely necessary when you were the only female ruler in all the Kingdoms, and you had rulers like Loris and Rodric constantly badgering you with demands.

"Gregory, did you hear what I just said?" Sarelle studied him with a quizzical expression.

"Yes, of course I did, Sarelle."

Gregory told himself to not let his mind stray again. He was too old to allow his mind to wander down certain paths.

His response didn't convince Sarelle. She continued nonetheless. "As I was saying, the Kingdoms have been fairly equal in power for the last thousand years. Many have schemed with or against one another, but never to any real end other than an occasional small shift in a border or more favorable trading rights. Yet, I fear that might be changing."

Gregory liked the way Sarelle's face lit up when discussing a matter of import, as she was doing now. He quickly caught what he was doing and reminded himself once again to focus.

"I've heard a number of disturbing possibilities from my political advisors regarding Rodric's actions and demands. Already he holds Loris in his hand. And I have my suspicions that Inishmore might be next. Rodric may be arrogant and conceited, but he's no fool."

"I agree with you on that," said Gregory. Though he was distracted, his acuity for politics remained sharp. He cut right to the chase, knowing where Sarelle was leading him. "I have seen many of the same signals as you have. Rodric is up to something, and none of it good for the rest of us I'm sure. Yet even now, in a time of supposed enlightenment where politics rules the day, power still is very much a physical manifestation. If Rodric, or Loris for that matter, tries to exercise that power in a way detrimental to Benewyn, Fal Carrach will stand with you."

Sarelle clapped her hands in pleasure, her smile lighting up her face. For a brief moment, Gregory thought his heart might stop.

"Gregory, you know exactly how to win a girl's heart." Gregory blushed at her words, something that she found quite appealing.

"We've been friends for quite a long time, Sarelle —

Benewyn and Fal Carrach — and our nations depend on each other for trade. Whatever Rodric may have in mind, it will not succeed in the east. And if I have my way, it will not succeed anywhere else either."

"Thank you, Gregory. You've calmed my fears."

Done with the day's business, Sarelle's smile subtly changed, becoming almost predatory. Gregory had the distinct feeling that he was the prey.

"You know, Gregory, a few months ago I was speaking with Lorena."

"Really," said Gregory, not pleased by that at all. He sighed heavily and sank back into his chair, knowing in which direction the conversation turned, and it was not to his favor. "What did the Queen of Kenmare have to say?"

Sarelle eyed Gregory with a knowing look. "She seems to think that you are in desperate need of a companion — at least I think that was the term she used."

Gregory wished he could sink even further into his chair. His mind searched for ways to escape the current conversation, but to no avail. He imagined he was locked in the dungeon and the jailer had thrown away the key. His breath came in short gasps, and a trickle of sweat ran down his chest. Sarelle leaned forward, effectively sealing the trap and giving Gregory an excellent view of her ample cleavage. He immediately looked away, but visions of that soft, white skin remained with him despite his best efforts.

"Yes, well, she has said much the same thing for quite a long time."

"Yes, she has," agreed Sarelle. "After much thought, though, I find that I now think she is right. A man of your stature really needs a wife. It must be difficult ruling a kingdom and raising a daughter at the same time."

Sarelle reached over and took hold of his hand, gently stroking it with her own. Though her voice remained soft, her eyes were sharp and flinty. Gregory felt as if he were surrounded by legions of enemy soldiers. In fact, he would have preferred it. He wiped his brow with his free sleeve.

"Having a wife could be a very practical decision, you know. Benewyn and Fal Carrach have always gotten along well together. Perhaps we should consider cementing the relationship in some way."

Sarelle looked at him expectantly, her hand still rubbing his own, her breath caressing his cheek. He had not seen it coming, even though he had once thought he could smell out a trap from miles away. He had no experience, though, in dealing with a woman of Sarelle's abilities, and he was having a hard time concentrating as he wiped his brow clean of sweat once more. Sarelle was so beautiful and had all the qualities and more that he looked for in a woman. But he had never considered being with anyone else after his wife died. Sarelle waited patiently for his response, but he had absolutely no idea what to say.

Much to his relief, the door to the outer chamber of the suite slammed open. Sarelle immediately sat back in her chair, releasing Gregory's hand. He glanced quickly at her eyes. He had escaped this time, if barely. Sarelle's smile promised that he would not be so lucky next time. What had he gotten himself into?

His worries immediately disintegrated. Kaylie stood in the doorway, a trail of water following after her. Her hair was matted down and her clothes were sopping wet. She looked as if she might collapse right there. Gregory went to her immediately, taking her into his arms, Sarelle right behind him. The tears that had threatened since Kaylie returned to the Palace finally burst free as she sobbed into her father's shoulder for several minutes.

Gregory simply held her, doing what he could to comfort his daughter. Sarelle went to a small table in the corner and poured a glass of wine. When the tears finally subsided somewhat, she made Kaylie drink to help calm her nerves.

"What happened, Kaylie?"

Gregory's concern was apparent. It was not normal for his daughter to break down in such a way.

Kaylie began her story, starting from when she met Thomas in the forest for the first time after the archery competition. Through muffled sobs and more tears she got it all out. When she was done, she felt completely drained, as if all her energy had exited with her words. Sarelle led her over to one of the chairs, pulling it closer to the fire so Kaylie wouldn't catch a chill from her drenched clothes.

"This is the same boy who helped us in the Burren and Oakwood Forest? You're certain of it?"

Gregory's words were soft and comforting, but his eyes churned with anger. Kaylie nodded that it was. If not for that boy, they would both be dead, their bones picked clean by those monstrous Fearhounds.

"And you're certain that he is from the Highlands?"

"Yes," answered Kaylie with some difficulty. Sarelle wrapped an arm around her shoulder, offering some comfort. "I can't let him die, father. I can't! Rodric is going to kill him. I could see it in his eyes. I can't let it happen."

Kaylie broke down into another bout of tears, this time using Sarelle's shoulder as her pillow. Gregory watched his daughter's agony, his insides twisting up in anger. First, because he could do nothing to take away his daughter's pain. Second, for the way Rodric had used her.

He kneeled down in front of her, taking her shivering hands in his own. "Don't fear, Kaylie. I will do everything I can to prevent it. This boy has done quite a bit for us. If I can do something for him in return, I will." He stood up once more and strapped on his sword before walking to the door.

"Will you stay with her, Sarelle?"

The Queen of Benewyn nodded as she hugged Kaylie to her chest. Gregory smiled in gratitude then slipped out into the hallway. His expression darkened as he strode toward the throne room. He may not understand women, but this new situation was something Gregory did understand. It was time to go to battle.

30

A SMALL CHANCE

The slam of the door against the wall reverberated throughout the throne room, startling its occupants. Gregory strode like a hurricane about to break against the coast, ignoring the pleading chamberlain's attempts to allow the small man to announce his presence.

"You had no right to involve my daughter in your schemes!" snapped Gregory, stopping just a few feet from the dais. "Why did you take the boy, Rodric?"

Gregory's fiery countenance made him appear like a demon rising out of the depths of the darkest hole, his eyes tight, his face an angry red, his expression murderous.

Rodric turned slowly from where he stood on the dais, having once again tried to knock some sense into Loris' head. The King of Dunmoor had been lounging on his throne with one leg hanging over an arm when Gregory stormed in. Now he was crouched against the tall back of the throne, his feet on the seat and ready to take him elsewhere if Gregory reached for his sword.

Rodric noticed Gregory's hand on the hilt of his sword, almost itching for the chance to draw it. He suddenly realized that no one else was in the room except for him and Loris. The chamberlain had scurried away, not wanting to become involved in the situation about to unfold, and had closed the doors when he left.

"What is the meaning of this, Gregory?" yelled Loris shrilly. "How dare you—"

"Quiet, Loris. I have no bone to pick with you this day."

Gregory spoke quietly, his voice cold. His eyes were even colder. For once, Loris was smart enough to listen.

"Just what are you talking about, Gregory?"

On the outside, Rodric appeared calm and confident. On the inside, his heart was in his throat. He had never feared for his safety before. What fool would risk assassinating the High King? Perhaps not a fool. Perhaps another king — who could assume his place. Rodric gulped down his nervousness, though his hands began to shake ever so slightly.

"You know very well what I'm talking about," said Gregory. "You used my daughter to get to the boy. Why?"

Gregory stepped closer to the throne. Loris burrowed farther into the woodwork in response while Rodric took an involuntary step backwards.

"I assure you, Gregory, Kaylie was never in any danger. Ragin and a troop of soldiers were always within range to offer immediate assistance."

"Answer the question!" ordered Gregory.

He had promised himself that he would remain calm, collected, yet the more he thought about what had happened as he walked through the shabby halls of the Palace, the angrier he became. Rodric had used his daughter in one of his schemes. His daughter!

"We simply wanted to talk with him," said Rodric, trying desperately to defuse the tension.

He had never expected such a response as this from Gregory and was caught completely unawares. At the bargaining table, he had sat across from the King of Fal Carrach many times, yet had never seen such pure rage. It terrified him. He searched frantically for a way to recover.

"The boy, as you call him, is a murderer. He killed five of my men."

Gregory almost lunged up the steps, his sword halfway out of its sheath.

"You dare to put my daughter in such danger!"

Rodric jumped back a few more feet, almost falling off the dais in his haste. "Let me explain, Gregory. Let me explain."

He walked back around the dais so that Loris, who remained sitting in the throne, was now the closest target for Gregory's wrath.

"They spent most of the afternoon of the archery competition together and got along fabulously from what I hear. They're friends. And as I said, with Ragin and a troop of soldiers nearby, she was never in any real danger, at least none she had not placed herself in."

Rodric was confident that his lie would hold. Chertney had assured him that Kaylie wouldn't remember anything until the magic wore off.

"Why do you want the boy, Rodric?"

"My dear Gregory. As I said, he killed five of my men. We suspected that he might be a criminal, so we wanted to talk to him. The boy chose to fight, an almost sure sign of guilt. I should think that you, of all people, a man known for his belief in the law, would understand my desire to prevent a person such as this Thomas from performing more mischief. If the boy had spoken with Ragin none of this would have happened."

"What proof do you offer with respect to the boy?"

Gregory examined the High King through slitted eyes, wondering if killing him now was worth the risk. Probably not, since Loris' soldiers outnumbered his own twenty to one.

"He killed five of my men when Ragin tried to talk with him. I think that's all the proof we need, don't you?"

Loris nodded mutely. He had heard all he needed to send the boy to the gallows. Of course, he'd agree to anything at the moment to get Gregory out of the room.

"Yes, I'm quite sure it was as innocent as you say," said Gregory doubtfully. "From what I understand Ragin never tried to talk. Why bother when the person you're seeking to speak to has been drugged."

"I assure you, Gregory, each of my men, to the man, would confirm my words. Thomas attacked them first and killed five of my men before they could subdue him."

"That's what worries me, Rodric. That's what worries me." Gregory stepped back from the dais, once again in control of his anger. "Soldiers have been known to say what their lord expects, rather than the truth."

Rodric's face turned flaming red, Gregory's insult biting deeply. No one could say such things to him. No one! Then he remembered that he and Loris were still alone in the throne room, and neither had a weapon. It was quite some time before Rodric responded as he struggled to control his temper. His mind worked at a furious pace, looking for a way to extricate himself from this mess while still achieving his primary goal — eliminating Thomas.

"I understand your concern for justice," said Rodric malevolently, "so perhaps there is another way to settle this matter if you doubt the integrity of my soldiers."

Rodric walked around the throne to stand in front of Gregory.

"Men or women accused of a crime have long been given the opportunity to prove their innocence through a test. Is that not correct?"

Rodric stared at Loris, waiting for a response. The King of Dunmoor, an unwilling spectator for so long, suddenly realized the ridiculous posture he had assumed in his fear. He placed his feet on the floor and assumed a normal sitting position, smoothing out his clothes as if nothing had occurred. It was wasted effort, but he did it nonetheless.

"Yes, that is correct, Rodric. In fact, we often use the Trial here in Dunmoor, all in the name of justice of course." Loris viewed such trials as sport and enjoyed them immensely.

"Perhaps you could fill us in, then, Loris. The accused is harbored in your dungeon, so according to the laws followed by all the Kingdoms, you are the rightful one to pass judgment on him."

Loris sat up straighter in his chair, warming to the subject. He did so enjoy the Trial. They were always quite entertaining. He cleared his throat before beginning.

"According to the law of Dunmoor there is a choice. The accused can be judged by the king — me — or can face the Trial. The choice is his. If he survives the Trial, then he goes free. If he doesn't survive, well, then justice has been done, as they say."

Gregory tried to remember just what form the Trial took here in Dunmoor, not having had cause to examine such things since he was a boy, when as part of his training as a prince, he was required to know the law not only in Fal Carrach, but in every other Kingdom as well. There was something about the Dunmoorian Trial that was unique. What was it?

As he thought about it, switching his gaze from the smirk on Rodric's face to the look of expectation and hope on Loris', he remembered with some distaste the choice available to him. No one had ever survived the Trial in Dunmoor. But then again, if Loris was allowed to pass judgment, the decision would be swifter, and more certain — death. At least with the Trial, the boy would stand a fighting chance. It was the best Gregory could do for him.

"The Trial, then," Gregory reluctantly agreed, hoping he

had not consigned the boy to a fate worse than the swift end provided on the headsman's block.

Loris grinned from ear to ear, just like a child who had received a candy from his mother.

"I bow to the wishes of my brother ruler," said Loris. "The boy will not be judged. Let him have a say in his own survival. He will face the Labyrinth" — Loris laughed shrilly — "and challenge the Makreen."

Rodric nodded his approval. It was not the way he originally wanted it to end, but it didn't really matter. The result would be the same.

31

FRUSTRATIONS

Gregory returned to his chambers, the events of the past hour running through his mind as he looked for some way to improve the boy's situation. He shook his head in frustration. In the end, he could think of nothing. He could only be satisfied that Thomas would have at least a chance at freedom. As he entered his apartments, Sarelle and Kaylie were still where he had left them. His daughter had fallen into a fitful slumber, her head resting comfortably on the Queen of Benewyn's lap.

"The Trial?" asked Sarelle.

Gregory nodded.

"I had expected as much," she said.

Their eyes locked for a moment, both thinking the same thing. Why was Rodric so desperate to kill the boy?

32

A TEST

Chertney glided down the steps silently, his feet barely scraping the stone. He welcomed the darkness surrounding him, relishing its touch. Several minutes passed before a light finally appeared at the bottom of the steps. Most people avoided the dungeon at all costs, but Chertney was not most people, not anymore. Rather, the dank and cold of the stone walls, the emptiness, made him feel as if he were home. And in a way, he was.

He walked down the passageway until he came to the last cell in the block, which shed a bright light out into the hallway. He smiled as he entered, excited by what was about to happen, something he had not had the opportunity to do in a very long time.

"Lord Chertney, we were expecting you," said a tall soldier, his long black hair sticking out from the back of his helmet. His hand was never far from the hilt of his sword and his mannerisms spoke volumes about his ability as a fighter. Chertney approved. At least some of Rodric's men appeared to know what they were doing. "The prisoner awaits you."

"Thank you, Captain Krayjak."

Chertney looked past the soldier to where his entertainment for the evening waited. The boy with blazing green eyes stood in the center of the room, his legs and arms chained to the stone floor. Around him stood twenty soldiers, many looking at the prisoner as if they held the Shadow Lord himself. The story of Thomas' capture had spread quickly and none of the soldiers currently on guard wanted to share in their comrades' fate. Hence their vigilance.

"You and your men may go now. I will tell you when to return."

"But, Lord Chertney," the tall captain protested, remembering Rodric's specific instructions about staying with the prisoner at all times. He did not want to be a victim of the High King's wrath.

Chertney looked at the soldier through cold eyes. Sometimes you had to know when to disobey your superiors, unfortunately a trait not common among soldiers.

"Tell me, Captain, who do you fear more — Rodric or me?"

The captain stared into Chertney's black eyes — and saw nothing. He gulped and immediately made the most important decision of his life.

"You, sir."

"An excellent choice," said Chertney. "Now leave us. You will know when I am done."

The captain quickly herded his men out of the room, all of whom were more than willing to take their leave.

Chertney waited until he was certain that the soldiers were well on their way back to the upper levels of the Palace before turning toward the boy. He was an anomaly. Neither big, nor physically imposing. He had won the archery contest and easily killed five men before sheer numbers prevented his escape. Well, that and the drug that had entered his system. Otherwise, he probably would still be free. Yet in those burning green eyes there was a strength, a purpose and a genuine confidence usually lacking in someone so young.

At the same time Thomas studied the man who stood before him. Thankfully, the drug had worn off for the most part. His vision had cleared, and he had regained his senses, though a splitting headache confirmed it would be quite awhile before the full effects of the drug left his body. He examined the midnight black clothes, the short hair and beard, the lifeless eyes, and even more important, the smell. Pure evil wafted over him, kicking the breath out of his lungs. An evil darker than any he had ever encountered.

Thomas was immediately on his guard. Lord Chertney was a dangerous man. The overwhelming stench of evil confirmed Thomas' worst fears. Chertney was close to the Shadow Lord. Thomas thought he might be a warlock, but the sensation wasn't quite right for that. The evil of a warlock was more subdued. Chertney's was more direct and aggressive. Thomas assumed that Chertney was a step above, perhaps even a few steps above, a warlock in the Shadow Lord's chain of command. And if that were true, he would have great skill in Dark Magic. Thomas would have to tread very carefully.

Guessing what was to come next, Thomas immediately cleared his mind. He stared straight ahead, ignoring Chertney, imagining that he was actually part of the stone wall in front of him. At first, the remnants of the drug in his body hindered his attempts. With some effort, though, he was finally able to achieve his goal. Soon he could feel the grainy touch of the wall, the harshness of its surface, its strength, flow into him.

"In the morning you will be given the chance to prove your innocence," announced Chertney, standing directly in front of Thomas with no more than a finger's breadth separating them. "To be honest, though, you have no hope of escape. One way or the other you will die. I could make things much easier for you, you know. All you have to do is answer a few questions for me."

Thomas felt what seemed like a cold hand run down his spine, and he shivered at its touch. Chertney attempted to probe his mind. He could feel the gentle touches at the edge of his consciousness, looking for an opening, a way to extract the knowledge locked away. Thomas focused even more on the stone walls, imagining he was physically pushing himself into it.

"I could kill you now," said Chertney, his stale breath caressing Thomas' face. "But then Rodric would not be able to have his fun. It would be much easier if you answered my questions. If you do, I promise you will feel no pain."

Chertney looked at Thomas hopefully, but not really expecting the boy to respond. If he truly was a member of the Sylvana, his defenses against Chertney's magic would be strong. His brief examination suggested that there was nothing remarkable about the boy, so perhaps the Sylvana accepted him because of his fighting skills. His reputation certainly made that the most likely possibility. If this boy had any skill in the Talent, Chertney would have known by now.

"How many of you are left, boy?"

Chertney walked around the circular cell, running a hand against the chains hanging from the ceiling. Thomas stared straight ahead, keeping the image of the wall in his mind. The pressure increased as Chertney searched for a breach in his defenses. All Chertney needed was a crack, a tiny crack, and he would be able to drain Thomas of whatever information he wanted. Thomas gritted his teeth in response, concentrating entirely on the wall. He could feel the gritty surface on his skin and taste the cragginess of the rock.

"There can't be many of you left," continued Chertney. "Are you still preparing for the return of the Shadow Lord?"

Chertney stopped for a moment to examine Thomas, then resumed his leisurely walk around the cell. A strong one indeed. Chertney increased the pressure of his mental probing and was rewarded with the sight of a few drops of sweat popping onto the boy's forehead. Chertney was reaching the limit of his strength in the Dark Magic. If he didn't break through soon, he never would.

Thomas' body shook slightly because of the effort. It felt as if a hundred blacksmiths armed with mallets were trying to pry open his skull. The incessant pounding rattled his mind, making it harder and harder for him to maintain his focus. Desperately he tried to hold on, knowing that the slightest wavering in his defense would spell the end.

If Chertney discovered his skill in the Talent, Chertney would kill him in an instant. Thomas bit down on his lip, hoping the immediate pain would help him maintain his quickly shattering concentration. Much to his relief, the physical pain allowed him to grasp some of the strands that threatened to unwind, and he held on to his defenses by his fingernails.

"You know, this time, you won't be so lucky. Are you planning to meet us at the Breaker once again?"

Chertney stopped abruptly, feeling how close he was to victory. The shell was about to crack. He redoubled his efforts, putting all of his remaining strength into tearing down Thomas' defenses.

Thomas dropped to his knees from the strain and closed his eyes in pain. His head felt like it was about to break apart. Chertney had chiseled his way through his defensive barrier to the very last layer, and even that was beginning to bend. Clenching his teeth in anger, he refused to concede victory.

The pressure continued to push down on him, pressing until it seemed that it would never end. Then miraculously it did. Thomas raised his head and quickly rebuilt the defenses in his mind. Thomas expected a final attempt from the warlock, but it never came. The dull ache in the back of his head became the constant hammering of a hundred hammers. Chertney stood over him now, his frustration plain.

"You have surprised me, boy. I thought you would have weakened, but obviously you have learned your lessons well. The Sylvana made an excellent decision. A pity you will be leaving their ranks come tomorrow."

Chertney walked toward the door, not bothering to look back at Thomas.

"Of course, if they have taken someone as young as you for a member, they must be in desperate straits indeed." Chertney laughed softly. "My master certainly will be pleased to hear that. It will make things that much easier for him."

Chertney stepped out into the hallway and made his way to the steps leading back up to the main floor of the Palace. This boy was an enigma. He would have enjoyed studying him longer, but judging from the determination he had just shown, it would have taken days to break through his defenses, and Chertney did not have days. Ah, well. He still had learned a few things that might prove useful, and come morning, there would be one less Sylvan Warrior to worry about.

As soon as Thomas was certain that Chertney had left, he collapsed on the cool stone floor, letting go of his defenses and drinking in the quiet of the cell. He had almost failed. Almost. The pounding in his head moved to its own rhythm, but Thomas no longer cared. He was completely drained, all of his energy spent on this single task. He soon fell into a fitful slumber, even with the pain drumming in his head. After what had just happened, nothing planned for the next morning could be any worse. Could it?

33

RECRIMINATION

Kaylie dabbed out the tears that threatened to form in her eyes once again. It seemed like she had been crying forever, yet it had only been a few hours since she had returned to the Palace. After her father told her Thomas' fate, she had run into her room and shut the door, not able to bear another person's company. She felt evil and corrupt, not wanting to be around others. Falling onto her bed she had cried into her pillow for several long minutes until the discomfort of wearing wet clothes forced her to change.

It was then that she decided she wasn't going to cry anymore, so she had instead tried to think of some way to help Thomas. She was responsible for his capture. She should be the one to win his freedom. Yet, nothing came to mind. She had paced in front of her bed for the better part of an hour with nothing to show for it. She had finally come to the conclusion that if her father couldn't succeed, how could she?

Still, she had to do something. The thought of Thomas hating her made her sick to her stomach. She had to apologize, to explain what had happened. She would not ask for his forgiveness — she didn't deserve that — but she would at least tell him the truth. Now if only these tears would cooperate so she could be about her business.

Bolstering her courage, she wiped her eyes a final time, threw down the handkerchief, and stormed out of her room. She was glad to see that her father had left for the moment, probably to walk Sarelle back to her chambers. Just to be sure, though, she stepped across the rich carpet and out through the main door on silent feet. There she nodded a greeting to the two soldiers standing guard and then trotted down the hallway before they could ask where she was going.

It didn't take her long to reach her destination, as no one was about because of the dreadful weather. Yet when she entered the anteroom that led to the dungeon, she was surprised to see approximately twenty soldiers milling about. She stopped for a moment, thinking on what to do, before finally deciding to charge forward.

"Princess. How are you this evening?"

A tall soldier with long black hair blocked her path. He was almost handsome, except for the sharpness in his eyes. She guessed that he was the leader of this troop.

"I'm fine, Captain." She adopted her stately tone, one that demanded respect. "Now if you will excuse me, I am here to see the prisoner."

The captain laughed softly, as did several of his men. "I'm sorry, Princess. That won't be possible. No one is allowed in the dungeon without the express permission of the High King."

"I am the Princess of Fal Carrach, Captain." She drew herself into a regal pose. "No one, not even the High King, can tell me what I can and cannot do."

The captain looked uncomfortable for a brief moment, then regained his nerve. That may be true, but then again, the Princess of Fal Carrach was of little consequence compared to the High King when in Dunmoor. Or, to put it in sharper perspective, when compared to Chertney.

"I'm sorry, but even you must obey his command, Princess. The High King was most specific. Besides, Lord Chertney is with the prisoner now. I don't think he wants to be disturbed. And I, for one, would not want to be the one to do so."

Lord Chertney! Kaylie thought she might get sick right there. She had only seen Chertney once, and then from a distance, but his very presence had sent a shiver of fear through her. A feeling of dread settled within her. What had she done?

"I see," she said, struggling to retain her dignity. "You will hear more of this, Captain."

She quickly turned on her heel and strode out of the room, not wanting to hear the chuckles of laughter she expected would follow her.

As she walked back through the Palace to her apartments, she promised herself that she would not cry again, though her tears threatened to become a waterfall. She barely remembered the conversation she had with Ragin the night before, having just returned from her time with Thomas.

It was all hazy, and though she tried to recall what was said, she could grasp nothing substantial within her mind. How could she have believed ill of Thomas? How could she have done this to him? He had been a friend to her, had saved her life twice before, and the life of her father, and this was how she repaid him? She had never felt so utterly horrible.

Caught up in her own thoughts, she collided with someone coming from a different direction. She almost fell, but a strong hand gripped her arm, steadying her. She was about to offer her thanks when she saw who it was. She immediately pulled her arm from his grasp.

"No thank you?" asked Ragin in mock surprise. "I expect better of you, Kaylie. I've always been impressed by your excellent manners."

"Leave me alone, Ragin, or I'll gut you like a fish."

Kaylie's anger consumed her. She placed her hand on her

dagger. Ragin took a few judicious steps backwards. He knew how good she was with a blade, and in her current state, her anger just might get the better of her.

"You did an excellent job earlier today, Kaylie," he said, not realizing the effect of his words. "Magnificent! You have done a great service for us all. Perhaps tomorrow, when the weather clears, we could go for a walk in the garden and I could thank you personally."

Kaylie stood there for a moment, her mouth open in shock. Had she heard him correctly? Was he really such a fool? Because of him Thomas was imprisoned. Yet the bastard was still trying to have his way with her? The world would freeze over before that happened. Her anger returned tenfold.

"Why do want him so badly, Ragin? Because he bested you at the Festival? Are you really so petty?"

Ragin's face slowly changed, becoming more arrogant and calculating. His lips curled into a sneer.

"I will be High King one day, Kaylie. I suggest you speak in a gentler tone."

"In name, perhaps," cut in Kaylie. "But never in deed. You are too small a man for that. Why did you want him captured?"

"My father considered him to be a threat," he said, not offering any detail. "So I took care of it. My father gets what he wants, and so do I."

He stepped forward menacingly, forcing Kaylie back up against the wall. The look in his eyes frightened her.

"Whether he's a murderer or not doesn't matter. His death has no meaning to me. He will die tomorrow, Kaylie. That will be the end of it, so I suggest you resign yourself to his fate."

Kaylie tried to get by Ragin, desperately wanting to be away from him. He reached for her arm and grabbed hold, then pulled her close.

"I have used you once, Kaylie, and I will again if necessary. There will come a time when you won't be able to say no."

"If that time comes, Ragin, I will choose death," she said harshly.

Remembering something Kael had taught her, she stomped down as hard as she could. Ragin danced back in pain with a curse, her heel having connected squarely with his shin. Not bothering to look back, she ran down the hallway. She didn't stop until she made it back to her apartments. That night, as sleep escaped her, one question kept running through her mind: *What have I done?*

34

PARTING GIFT

"**G**et up, you misfit. Get up I say!"

The voice penetrated the darkness consuming Thomas, sealing him away from the world and the pain. The hard kick to his midsection forced him from his sleep and back to where his aches and injuries ruled.

"Get up, scum. It's time for the day's entertainment, and you're to be the main act." The guard laughed harshly, his large belly shaking with mirth.

"Bring him, Sergeant. We don't have time to waste this morning."

"Yes, sir," said the sergeant hastily. Captain Krayjak was a strict one and not to be crossed. "Put these on and be quick about it."

Thomas struggled to open his eyes. He quickly closed them again, as even the dim light of the cell sent shooting pains through his skull. He shifted his weight and pushed himself into a seated position, which set off a pounding in his temple.

His mental skirmish with Chertney the night before was the hardest battle he had ever fought, though it left no visible wounds. Mustering what strength remained, he forced the pain that threatened to overwhelm him to the back of his mind. The constant hammering became a dull ache at the edge of his awareness. He sensed that he would need all his senses and skills to survive the day ahead. The aches and pains would have to wait for another time.

"Quickly, scum. Quickly I said!" The sergeant towered over him, his huge paunch blocking out the little light provided by the torch jammed into the wall by the cell door. The sergeant made a threatening gesture with his foot. "Let's get a move on. Otherwise you'll be eating my foot for breakfast."

Without thinking, Thomas grabbed the foot dangling in front of his face with two hands and shoved the fat man away from him. The sergeant tumbled backwards, his head slamming against the stone of the far wall, the dull thud echoing throughout the small chamber.

It took a few moments for the sergeant to realize what had happened to him. Rubbing the back of his head, his face twisted into a mask of rage. He was on his feet quicker than any would expect for someone of his size.

"Why you little beggar! Now you're in for a beating that you'll never—"

"Enough, Sergeant." Krayjak placed himself between his subordinate and Thomas, his eyes holding no emotion, though the other soldiers in the cell had clearly enjoyed the spectacle. "No more games."

"Yes, sir," replied the sergeant, bowing his head in submission, though his anger remained. The little scum would get his soon enough.

The captain turned toward Thomas, who remained sitting calmly on the floor of the cell.

"Put the training gear on. We leave in two minutes. You either wear the gear or nothing at all."

The captain pulled a key from his belt and unlocked the ankle chains holding Thomas in place. Then he walked to the door and waited, showing no concern whatsoever as to what Thomas chose to do.

It was a simple decision really. Thomas examined what the sergeant had thrown at him — a pair of training shorts and a baggy shirt. The pieces of clothing resembled some of the attire worn by the gladiators of old. For hundreds of years they fought for sport, winning and losing the fortunes of those gambling on them. Eventually, such practices were outlawed, though it was rumored that in some isolated areas on the continent the Games, as they were called, continued.

Thomas rose to his feet and quickly changed his clothes, having some problems pulling off his torn shirt and putting on the one provided by the captain because of the chains attached to his wrists. He was about to pull on his boots as well.

"You won't be needing those," said Krayjak. "Leave them here."

Thomas shrugged, not really caring. He had no idea what was about to happen to him, though he was certain it wasn't going to be pleasant.

"Come along," said the captain, motioning him through the door.

Thomas shuffled after him, his legs slow to respond to his commands. It took him several steps to finally get his feet under him again. When he stepped out into the hallway, he was met by twenty soldiers, ten on each side, who formed up around him. Krayjak moved to the front, the sergeant taking a place directly behind Thomas. The captain then barked a command and the troop began its trek to the main floors of the Palace.

It was slow-going through the passageway leading to the steps, though Thomas didn't mind. It gave him a chance to work the kinks out of his muscles. The manacles on his wrists remained, a soldier on each side holding onto a chain. Even with twenty men, the captain wasn't taking any chances.

The group began its journey up the steps with Thomas doing his best to keep up. His legs were still weak and it was taking awhile to get the blood flowing again. They were halfway up when he felt a boot connect with the small of his back, knocking him forward. His head slammed into the step just behind the captain, his chained hands preventing him from protecting against the blow.

Thomas lay there in a daze, the pain he had locked away coming back tenfold, now accompanied by a distant ringing. Blood trickled down his forehead. The stone had opened a long gash above his right eye.

Krayjak looked down at his prisoner, then turned harsh eyes on the sergeant. There was no feeling there, only purpose and duty. The sergeant gulped as his captain's gaze bored into his very soul.

"He tripped, Captain. I tried to catch him, but I wasn't quick enough."

Sweat poured from the sergeant, and not just because of the arduous climb up the steps. Perhaps he had crossed the line this time. He had seen what his captain did to those men who disobeyed him. Swallowing nervously, he considered that possibility. Krayjak held the sergeant's gaze for a moment longer before looking down at his prisoner.

"Bring him," he said, then he headed back up the steps.

The two soldiers who held Thomas' chains pulled him to his feet. He stumbled up the first few steps before regaining his balance. Blood poured down his head, trickling over his eye and the side of his face and then soaking into his shirt. Just a flesh wound, thankfully. But with his hands held at his sides, he could do nothing to stanch the flow.

Thomas marched along with the soldiers, forgetting the cut on his forehead for a moment to do something about the pounding in his temple. This time it took even more effort to lock away the pain. Still, it was the best he could do in his current physical condition. He then tried to wipe his face on his shirt, but found that it wasn't very effective. Resigned to his predicament, he trudged along, wondering what was to come next.

35

THE LABYRINTH

Once the troop reached the main level of the Palace, they marched down a long hallway that stretched into the horizon. As the minutes passed, Thomas barely glanced at the tapestries and frescoes dotting the walls. Instead, he focused on the large bronze doors that grew larger with each step. He could hear the murmur of many voices gradually increasing in intensity as they approached the massive doors.

Thomas tried to clear his throat, but it was too dry, and he wished desperately for a drink of water. A premonition of danger filled him and his instincts automatically took over. He looked for a way to escape, his eyes darting from side to side. The captain sensed his anxiety, as did his men. They tightened up their formation, and the two soldiers strengthened their grips on his chains. There was nowhere for him to go. Nowhere at all, except through the doors now standing straight and tall in front of him.

The captain stepped up to the bronze door on the right. Grabbing hold of a large knocker that resembled the grotesque head of a goblin, he slammed it against the bronze, the sound echoing back down the hallway. Three times the captain pounded on the door. The murmurs behind the doors died down to absolute silence.

Satisfied with some result that Thomas could not discern, the captain motioned to two of his men, who ran forward and took hold of the door handles. Tensing their bodies, they pulled against the massive weight of the doors. At first, the doors wouldn't move. Then slowly, ever so slowly, they were pulled apart and pushed back against the wall. The captain walked across the threshold, his soldiers following right behind him with Thomas in their midst.

Thomas' mouth opened in surprise as he walked into what resembled a small stadium. He had been right about his clothes. A gladiator's pit appeared before him. The soldiers walked him halfway into the room until he stood in front of a square opening in the floor just large enough for a man to squeeze through. The soldiers then moved away from him and formed up into two even columns. The large bronze doors were pulled shut.

The captain then approached, a key in hand. Releasing Thomas from his shackles, he stepped away as well. Thomas immediately checked the wound on his forehead. The flow of blood was now a trickle. He dabbed at it with the collar of his shirt before examining his new surroundings.

The gladiator's pit was just beyond the opening in the floor. Bright white sand covered the floor and the walls, made of smooth, white marble, were at least twenty feet high. Dark, almost black, splotches dotted its length, testifying to its harsh and deadly use. It didn't take much to figure out how the spots had gotten there.

Silently he thanked Rynlin and Rya for forcing him to focus on his lessons. Taking a deep breath to steady himself, he tried to prepare for what was to come. Looking away from the pit in an effort to settle his nerves, he glanced up, then realized he had completely ignored the most obvious feature of the arena — the gallery, which teemed with people.

Lords and ladies filled the rows of seats, all of whom stared back at him. He ran his gaze from one side to the other, unsettled by their staring eyes. More people watched him now than during the archery competition. He became distinctly nervous. They were judging him, weighing him with their eyes. He considered making a break for it, but he didn't think the soldiers standing behind him would appreciate the effort.

"Do you wish to proclaim your guilt? If so, the sentence will be carried out quickly."

Thomas stared straight ahead, the voice instantly putting him on alert. Across the wide expanse of the pit Rodric sat on a plush throne, his large, gaudy crown of gold tilting awkwardly on his head. On his right-hand side sat Ragin, and on his other Loris of Dunmoor. Thomas forgot his pain, his thoughts immediately turning to revenge. His eyes burned brightly, his anger hot. Realizing there was nothing he could do at the moment to release his hate, he glanced at the others in the gallery.

There was a pretty woman with long blonde hair sitting next to Ragin who returned his glance boldly. Gregory was there as well, sitting next to a very beautiful woman with auburn hair, but his mood was dark, almost murderous. Thomas' eyes continued along the row. His breath caught in his throat for a moment. Kaylie sat next to her father. From her appearance, he could see that she had been crying. Concern never materialized within him, however. She was the reason he stood there. She had betrayed his trust. He ignored her pleading eyes and turned his attention back to Rodric.

"Do you wish to proclaim your guilt?" Rodric had grown testy, patience not one of his virtues.

Thomas stood there quietly, ignoring the many people watching him. He stared straight ahead, locking eyes with Rodric, defiance in his gaze.

"With the evidence presented against you, you deserve the headsman's block," continued Rodric. "Yet our brother ruler from Fal Carrach asked for a different sentence. I was quite happy to agree to it."

Rodric looked over at Gregory. The King of Fal Carrach sat stiffly in his chair, holding Kaylie's hand in his own. He was obviously having some difficulty controlling his anger and chose instead to ignore Rodric. The High King didn't seem to mind.

"Therefore, we have decided to put you to the Trial rather than send you to the executioner. Let your actions determine your innocence. If you survive the maze, and the Makreen, you are free to go."

Rodric said the last part gleefully, clearly not believing that he would survive the ordeal.

Thomas continued to stare straight ahead until Rodric was forced to break eye contact. He had the urge to look at Kaylie one more time, but he stopped himself. He refused to show any weakness. Kaylie was not to be trusted, not ever again.

"Good luck, boy," said Rodric. "You will need it. You must survive on your wits alone. Are you sure you do not want to confess your guilt?"

Rodric waited almost a full minute for a response, the tension building in the arena as a low murmur began, but Thomas ignored him.

"So be it. The gladiators of old used to fight in their training shorts. The custom will continue today. Captain, remove his shirt."

Krayjak stepped forward, but one look from Thomas froze him. Thomas pulled the shirt over his head. Gasps of shock accompanied the movement. Gregory's face turned an angry red as he took in the scars of the whip crisscrossing his body, and Kaylie fought desperately to hold back her tears. She wanted to say something to him, anything, to take the betrayal from his eyes, but words failed her. She had failed him.

Thomas glanced around the arena a final time, then he turned back toward Rodric. He offered the High King a smile, one that turned Rodric's blood cold. His fate had been determined for him. So be it. There was no place to go but down. Before the captain could order his soldiers to force him through the hole, Thomas jumped through the opening into darkness.

As he did so, memories of his lessons with Rynlin and Rya flashed through his mind. Lessons of the Trials. One fact stood out from the others. No one had ever defeated the Makreen. No one had ever entered the labyrinth and lived.

36

GETTING HELP

T he howl drifted through the night, silencing the normal nighttime chatter heard along the Highland coast. Beluil waited expectantly on the sandy beach, having arrived a few hours before. Normally it would not have taken him two days to get from the western edge of Oakwood Forest to the eastern edge of the Highlands where it butted up against the Sea of Mist, but Thomas' sword slowed him down. Having gotten the blade into its sheath, he dragged it behind him with the strap in his teeth.

The black wolf looked out across the darkened waves toward the faint outline of the Isle of Mist half a mile away. He knew the residents of the island could hear him. He need only wait. But they needed to hurry. Too much time had already passed. Beluil howled again, a sharp, piercing cry that contained all of his sorrow.

Off to the west an answering howl drifted down from the Highlands, but Beluil ignored it. Another time he would have gone off to visit with the pack, but not tonight. He howled again, the cry echoing along the coast, trapped by the steep cliffs. He was about to try again, but his call was finally answered.

A large eagle streaked out of the darkened sky and landed on the sand in front of Beluil. The wolf turned away from the brief flash of bright white light that followed. When he turned back, Rynlin stood before him. He appeared somewhat bedraggled, his hair going in every direction.

"Where have you two been, Beluil?" asked Rynlin, his irritation clear. "Rya has been worried sick about the two of—"

Rynlin looked around quickly, a tremor of fear rising up from the pit of his stomach. Something was terribly wrong. "Where's Thomas?"

Beluil expected such a reaction from Rynlin. He motioned to the sand with his paw. Rynlin stepped forward and picked up the long, sleek object. Thomas' sword. He pulled it free of its sheath. The bright steel flashed in the faint light of the quarter moon, the black splotches covering much of its length visible.

Blood, relatively fresh. Rynlin's worry became a roiling ball in his stomach. Cursing his luck at not having Thomas' ability to speak with animals, he would have to use a more mundane method to communicate. At least Thomas wasn't dead. He would have known that thanks to the necklace.

In an instant Rynlin took hold of the Talent. He stretched it out to the west, extending his senses as far as he could. He didn't stop until he reached well into Dunmoor. Strangely he couldn't locate his grandson through the necklace, a fact that boded ill. His worry increased tenfold. A slow, burning rage began churning within him.

"Where did you last see him, Beluil?"

Beluil smiled, glad that Rynlin was so perceptive. He didn't want to waste any more time than necessary trying to explain the events of the past few days. They could be stuck there all night, and for Thomas, those precious hours could be crucial to his survival. Beluil turned around, facing toward the Highlands.

"To the west," said Rynlin.

Beluil whipped back around, barking an acknowledgement.

"The Highlands? Fal Carrach? Dunmoor?" Beluil barked again. Good, they were narrowing the search area down.

"The Strand?" That seemed the most obvious choice, yet Beluil did not reply.

"Oakwood Forest?" Beluil barked again. Rynlin's fear increased.

"Well done, Beluil," said Rynlin, slipping the strap of the scabbard over his shoulder. "Return to where you last sensed Thomas in Oakwood Forest. I'll meet you there before noon today."

Beluil bolted off despite his weariness, running at a furious pace to the west. He would do as Rynlin commanded. His brother was in danger and now he could finally offer his help.

Rynlin watched the wolf go. His anger threatened to overwhelm him, and he had to fight to control it. Now was not the time to lose his temper. He could do that after he found Thomas. But first, he had a feeling that he would need some help.

37

NEW ACQUAINTANCE

Thomas landed on the balls of his feet, crouching in the stillness of the pitch-black hole. Krayjak had closed the opening, eliminating the faintest trace of light. He shifted from side to side, listening, waiting for his vision to adjust. Slowly, the darkness changed, becoming more of a shadowy veil. He could understand why the Makreen never lost. Anyone without vision as good as his wouldn't stand a chance.

The Makreen could strike any time he chose with its prey none the wiser. After a few seconds, Thomas began to pick out his surroundings. Made of sharply cut stone, the high-ceilinged tunnel stretched on into the darkness. A thin layer of dust covered the floor, a testament to how long it had been since the labyrinth had last been used.

As he studied his new battleground, he thought back to one of his lessons with Rynlin. He could even remember his grandfather's pedantic tone. Rynlin was explaining how the Kingdoms used to put people through Trials to judge their innocence, based on the theory that if you survived, you had to be innocent. Thomas had lost interest in the lecture as Rynlin inevitably went down several tangential paths, so his mind had wandered. His grandfather had been holding onto a piece of paper, so Thomas decided to have a little fun.

Using the Talent, he set the piece of paper on fire, much to the surprise of his grandfather, who had dropped the burning parchment and leapt back, almost knocking his head on the low ceiling of the cottage. Of course, Rynlin had been furious, doubling Thomas' chores for a month as a result, but it had been worth it. Rynlin had muttered to himself for the rest of the day, angrier with himself for not sensing Thomas' use of the Talent than he was with Thomas for using it in such a manner.

Thomas pushed the memory away. He couldn't afford to let his mind wander now. He had to focus on his survival. No one had ever made it through the labyrinth alive. The Makreen didn't allow it.

If he remembered correctly, a thousand or more years in the past a tribe of Makreen had lived in the Charnel Mountains. But with the coming of the Shadow Lord, eventually he had subverted them. As the story went, even the Shadow Lord had miscalculated, though, as to their vicious nature. Over time the Makreen broke free from their yokes. No one had ever offered a satisfactory explanation on how such a thing could occur, but there was no denying that it had happened.

After escaping the grasp of the Shadow Lord, the Makreen left the Charnel Mountains and ravaged the Kingdoms. The Shadow Lord originally had conquered them for a single purpose, and a single purpose only — to kill. They were the elite troops in his armies, and they performed their duty with a savage pleasure, killing anything and everything they could, if only for the joy of it.

The Kingdoms hunted down the Makreen and had virtually succeeded in eliminating them as a threat, though at a terrible price. For every Makreen killed, ten men or more often perished because of the beasts' savagery and skill with weapons. Only a few survived, usually in the remote regions where men dared not go — and here in the Labyrinth, of course. Here where Thomas had no choice but to go forward.

With Thomas' eyes, it seemed like he was in a perpetual twilight, yet twilight was often the most dangerous time of the day in the forest, the time when many predators came out to hunt. About thirty paces down the passageway, it branched off to the left and the right. Thomas stepped forward quietly, placing his feet carefully. Silence reigned in the Labyrinth, so much so he felt like he walked in a tomb. His tomb. Coming to the fork, he peered down each hallway, looking for some sign of movement. Nothing. The only sound came from his own breathing.

Not knowing which way to go, he chose the left. He went slowly, treading softly on the stone floor. As he made his way through the tunnel, he had a feeling that he had forgotten something. That feeling continued to play in the back of his mind, nagging him with his every step. He didn't have time to ponder it.

Coming up on another intersection, a blur of movement and flash of steel caught his eye. Thomas dove to the floor, trying to evade the attack. He almost didn't make it. The attacker's blade slid across his ribs rather than through them. He immediately regained his feet and leapt backward, just in time to avoid another thrust from the sharp blade.

This wasn't working. Eventually his attacker would strike true. Thomas had to change his strategy, quickly.

The shadow in front of him lunged forward again. Thomas sidestepped the attack, but this time, instead of backing away, he moved forward. Reaching for the haft of the weapon, he ripped it from the hands of his surprised attacker, then jumped back, holding the blade in front of him to prevent another attack. Thomas saw shock register in the eyes of his opponent, yet only for a split second. As fast as the shadow had first appeared, it blended into the darkness and ducked back around a corner.

Still, his attacker was visible long enough for Thomas to get a good view of what he was up against, and it wasn't promising. The Makreen stood fully twelve feet tall. Green scales covered its heavily muscled torso and legs, its face resembling that of a goblin, with small, curling horns set atop its head.

Certain that the Makreen was no longer a threat, at least at the present time, Thomas examined the slash across his ribs. It was a painful wound, but the blade hadn't cut deeply. Still, blood dripped down his side and soaked his shorts, and he had nothing with which to stanch the flow.

He would have to continue and hope for the best. With the cut on his head and now the one on his side, his endurance could become a problem. And time was now an even bigger problem. The quicker he was out of the Labyrinth, the better.

Thomas' disposition brightened somewhat as he examined his newly acquired weapon. Quite impressive. Quite impressive indeed. At first he had thought it was a spear, but then realized his mistake. He had never seen a weapon quite like this one. It was actually a quarterstaff with a few nasty surprises, the most obvious being the slightly curved two-foot blades affixed to both ends.

Thomas smiled in admiration. It was slightly larger than what he was used to, as it had been made for a creature the size of the Makreen. Still, it was a weapon that he could certainly use. His chances for getting through the Labyrinth alive had just improved immeasurably. Now if only he could remember what still nagged at him.

Thomas hadn't expected the Makreen to run off so quickly, though it had clearly been surprised by Thomas' action. The beasts were known as fierce warriors, fear not being a part of their makeup. Then again, they were also known for playing with their prey and inflicting as much pain as possible before finishing them. Perhaps that was the tactic the Makreen had decided on.

Twirling the quarterstaff in his hands, Thomas continued back down the passageway, more confident, but wary of what was to come.

"I won't be easy meat," he whispered to himself. "I won't."

Besides, he refused to give Rodric the satisfaction of dying so easily.

38

FILLED WITH WORRY

Kaylie wrung her hands in fear and frustration, glancing every so often at the darkened doorway that led out from the Labyrinth to the pit just below her. She hoped to see Thomas leap out, victorious and free, yet with each passing second her fear of his demise increased.

When she wasn't looking for Thomas, she watched the nobility crowded into the gallery. The people around her made her sick. Everyone in the High King's gallery was talked gaily, making bets as to how long it would take the Makreen to finish Thomas off. The whole thing repulsed her. How could you bet on someone's life so callously? She simply couldn't understand it.

Her father remained at her side, patting her on the knee from time to time in an effort to provide some comfort. His expression was calm, but his eyes were grim. He clearly wasn't happy with what was going on, but he was not in a position to do anything about it.

Kaylie tried to take strength from her father, refusing to cry or show any other outward sign of weakness. But on the inside, she was in turmoil. Because of her Thomas was in the

Labyrinth. Because of her he was fighting the Makreen, one of the most gruesome beasts ever to walk the earth. Because of her, he would probably die.

She didn't think she could bear such a curse. She looked once again at the doorway leading out to the pit, but nothing emerged. Instead the darkness teased her, the opening resembling the maw of some ancient beast, grinning at her wickedly.

39

———

SURPRISE

T homas crept silently down the tunnel, not wanting to make even the slightest sound and alert the Makreen to his presence. Thomas' luck had held during the first attack. He hoped it would stay with him. As he made his way down the roughly cut tunnel, he tried to block away the new pain in his side.

The first skirmish with the Makreen had reopened the wound on his head, a small trickle of blood flowing down his face. The blood on his side had begun to congeal around the wound on his ribs, yet it would be a long time before it stopped bleeding completely. By then, if he didn't find something to wrap around it to stop the flow, he would probably be dead.

As the pain pushed against his awareness, Thomas' thoughts wandered. How could Kaylie have done this to him? His bitterness welled up within him. He had tried to be her friend and this was how she repaid him. Tricking him and then handing him over to Rodric. If he got out of this— Well, he didn't have time to think about the future. Not yet, anyway. He forced his thoughts back to the present.

As the minutes crept by, the buzz in the back of his head

continued to annoy him. There was something he was forget-ting, something important that escaped him during the Makreen's attack. He just couldn't dredge it out of his memory.

The tunnel finally came to an end. Yet this time there were three branches from which to choose. Which one should he take? There was nothing remarkable about either one, yet if he made the incorrect choice, he could end up wandering the Labyrinth until the Makreen caught him unprepared.

That was something he did not want to allow. He was tired of being hunted. It was time to reverse the roles. His anger flared anew as he considered his predicament once more. Unfortunately, he had no outlet for it, and his irritation offered little assistance in deciding which way to go.

A memory suddenly came to mind, one that had been buried within him for quite some time. He remembered being in the tunnel underneath the Crag, escaping from what had been his home. The tunnel and his anger had been much the same then. Wait a moment. Maybe there was a way he could improve his odds.

He had used the Talent, though somewhat awkwardly, while under the Crag. Perhaps he could do the same now. The Talent was often difficult to control in castles or towns because the stones used in their construction had been shaped by man, thereby eliminating some of their natural vitality. But here the stone remained intact for the most part, the tunnels having been carved from it. Maybe he could use that to his advantage.

Thomas reached for the Talent, the power flowing within him offering a renewed confidence. He suddenly realized, though, that he could not grasp as much as he desired. His struggle with Chertney the night before and his two recent injuries had sapped much of his physical and mental strength, two factors that played a large part in determining how much of the Talent he could wield at any one time.

What about Chertney? He was obviously a warlock, or

something worse. Would he be able to feel Thomas' power up in the gallery? Probably not, Thomas decided. The stone would hide it from him, and since Thomas could only manage a relatively small amount at the moment, he didn't think he had anything to worry about, except for finding a way out of the Labyrinth.

Thomas extended his senses, pushing the Talent into the stone. Much to his annoyance, it didn't go very far at all. Was he doing something wrong? He had done the same thing he always did when using it in the forest to — that must be it.

He smiled as understanding came to him. Rya had been adamant when teaching him how to master the Talent that he comprehend one point: You could do almost anything with the Talent, if you had the strength and necessary control, yet each environment required a slightly different approach. He had been handling the Talent the wrong way.

Thomas took a deep breath to steady himself, then tried again, this time adapting the Talent slightly to compensate for his current environment. Yes, that was it! The power flowed easily through the stone now. In a matter of seconds he had a map of the entire Labyrinth in his mind, showing him the dead ends and, more important, the exit. He saw every twist and turn clear as day.

Holding the image of the Labyrinth in his mind, he took the right passageway, still moving slowly, wary of a surprise attack. The Makreen had been gone too long, increasing Thomas' worry. As he walked down the passageway, Thomas twirled the two-bladed quarterstaff in front of him, expecting an attack at any moment. Yet there was only silence and no sign of movement up ahead.

The passageway changed somewhat as he walked along. It had a rougher cut here, with holes about the size of his palm running along the length of the wall where it met the floor. That was strange. He was about to shrug it off as the end of the hallway appeared up ahead when he suddenly stopped in his tracks. He had heard something scrape against the floor just off to his left, close to the base of the wall.

Thomas redirected the Talent, pulling in the power from the entire Labyrinth to focus it on the passageway he now stood in. He gulped nervously. He had spent too much time looking at the big picture rather than the details.

Of course there were holes in the wall here. How else were the rock vipers supposed to get into the tunnel? He extended his senses the length of the passageway. It was literally teeming with the small, extremely venomous snakes. They slithered up and down the sides of the tunnel, tentatively pausing every now and then in search of prey — in search of him, he realized.

Rock vipers were tiny compared to a bloodsnake, but they could be just as deadly. A single bite carried enough poison to kill a man in a matter of seconds. They lived in the darker recesses of the world, preying on mice, rats, moles, bats and the like that inhabited the caves and crevices dotting the earth. Because of the darkness of their habitat, they hunted by movement, sensing the reverberations of their prey as it moved along. And Thomas had walked right into their nest without even realizing it.

His first instinct was to make a run for it, thinking that he could get down the tunnel before one of the rock vipers struck. He lifted his foot slightly off the ground. The warning hiss of a snake kept his foot off the ground and sent a bolt of fear through him. He looked down with his eyes, not wanting to move his head. A rock viper was coiled up just a finger's breadth away from his bare foot. Thomas would be dead in seconds if he moved.

His mind worked furiously, desperately searching for some solution, yet nothing came to mind. A flash of movement caught his eye. The clink of a quarrel hitting the wall of the passageway just to his left greeted his ears, followed by the sound of several snakes striking out at the crossbow bolt when it fell to the stone floor.

Thomas looked for the source of the bolt, not surprised to see the Makreen standing at the end of the tunnel, no more than forty feet away, grinning wickedly at his prey's predicament. Thomas cursed himself for a fool. He should have remembered the traps! How could he have forgotten them?

During the entire time the Labyrinth had been used as a Trial, the stories about it focused on the exploits of the Makreen, yet the history books reported that most of the people sent into the Labyrinth died because of the traps, not the Makreen. That didn't make for as exciting a story, though, so the Makreen was always the main villain.

Thomas became almost frantic, his feet itching for the opportunity to escape. Yet he had nowhere to go. He could die either from the bite of a snake or the bolt of a crossbow. It was really no choice at all.

Shaking its massive head in pleasure at Thomas' situation, the Makreen raised the crossbow to his chin, sighting the crosshairs on Thomas' chest. Thomas watched in morbid fascination as the process of his death played out in front of him. He could think of nothing to do, nothing at all. A cold sweat began to drip down his back, causing a shiver along his spine. There had to be something. He had a weapon after all. He had to try something.

As Thomas saw the Makreen's finger close around the trigger of the crossbow, releasing the bolt, an idea finally came to him. Tensing his muscles, he jumped for the ceiling, driving the blade of the quarterstaff into the stone. The bolt passed right where Thomas had been, slicing through the snake that had sensed Thomas' movement and struck at him.

Thomas glanced down the passageway and breathed a sigh of relief. The Makreen was gone, for now. Maybe his luck was still with him after all. Yet, he still hadn't reached safety. How long the blade would remain in the ceiling he didn't know, and his movement had attracted several dozen more rock vipers, now slithering beneath him in anticipation.

Thomas held onto the quarterstaff with all his might, yet his sweaty palms were becoming a hindrance as he slowly slipped down its length inch by inch. His escape had only been momentary. And if he didn't think of something else quickly, it would become wasted effort all together.

As his right hand slid down to the middle of the quarter-staff, a slight indentation met his grip. Pressing in on it, his ears were greeted by a quiet click. He smiled. Yes, his luck may be turning. Pulling with his right hand, the quarterstaff came apart in the middle, giving Thomas two small spears with which to work.

Checking the passageway once more to make sure the Makreen had not returned, Thomas began his journey along the roof of the tunnel, driving one blade after the other into the hard rock, steadily drawing closer to safety. Every movement racked his tortured body with pain, his muscles protesting from the strain and the wound in his side throbbing in defiance. He endured it, preferring the pain to the dreamy, endless sleep offered by the bite of a rock viper.

It was slow-going, but Thomas didn't want to risk missing the mark with a blade as he pulled himself across the ceiling. Finally, after several long minutes of struggle, he reached the end of his journey, pulling the blades free from the ceiling and dropping down to the floor safely away from the rock vipers. He had made it, if just barely. He took no comfort in his success, however. He had a feeling that his struggles had just begun.

40

PREMONITION

"So, Chertney, are you still concerned?" Rodric leaned back in his chair, twisting his head to speak to the man sitting directly behind him. "Do you really think the boy will make his way past the Makreen? In one thousand years a single man has never defeated a Makreen on his own."

Rodric looked from side to side, watching the lords and ladies in his gallery chatter excitedly about the probable outcome of the Trial. Most had agreed that it would be over within the hour — the boy was no match for the beast. Rodric tended to agree with them. But that time limit fast approached.

The forbidding shadow lurking behind the High King grimaced with distaste. How such a small and petty man could rule a kingdom he didn't know.

"If anyone could, it would be he," answered Chertney.

He had learned much from Thomas the night before, if only in terms of the boy's character. The boy's strength was obvious. Chertney had left Thomas with a vague sense of worry. If there were more like him waiting to defend the Kingdoms as they had in the past, his master's grand plan could be in jeopardy.

"You give the boy too much credit," said Rodric, not bothering to turn around this time. Instead he looked over at Gregory and his daughter.

The girl obviously wasn't taking this very well, and her father was furious. The latter filled him with glee. Gregory had hindered his plans for years. Now Rodric finally had the opportunity to return the favor.

"You should have killed him right away," replied Chertney, leaning down to whisper into Rodric's ear, his words coming out in a malevolent hiss.

Chertney had a bad feeling about the boy. The scars on his body proved his fortitude. Still, there was something else that bothered him about Thomas, but what? That's what worried him. Surprises tended to come back and haunt you, and Chertney was not in the position to take such a risk, not with a master such as his.

"Relax, Chertney. Relax and enjoy the fun. In just a few minutes you will have nothing to worry about. You will have your wish and the Makreen will have his kill."

Chertney looked down at the balding top of the High King, visible through the crown perched precariously on his head. Perhaps. Then again, perhaps not. Chertney's premonition of danger increased with each passing minute.

41

———

A SWIM

The click as Thomas pushed the two blades together to form the quarterstaff echoed down the passageway. Looking back the way he had come, Thomas was pleased to see that most of the rock vipers had returned to their holes once all movement ceased. He breathed deeply to steady himself. He was at a crossroads again and could go either right or left. The Makreen had disappeared, probably to plan his next attack. Thomas didn't want to give him too much time to think. He had to move faster.

The longer he was in the Labyrinth, the better his chances of dying — either by some trap or his own weakness. Extending his senses, the picture of the maze returned to his mind. Pinpointing his current location, he turned right. After walking down that tunnel, he turned right, then left, then right again. His senses were raw with anticipation as he searched for the Makreen, but the beast did not reappear, a fact that worried him.

As he continued on his way, the map of the Labyrinth became fuzzier in his mind. He was having a much harder time using his Talent through the rock. The tunnel had changed in appearance. The walls and floor were now made of blocks of stones, much like any hallway in the Palace above, which explained his difficulty with the Talent.

The stones grew increasingly bigger the farther he went down the passageway, until finally each one was large enough for a horse to comfortably stand on. Bending down, Thomas studied the floor, an odd feeling of danger passing through his mind. There were slight spaces between the blocks of stone that he could fit a finger through. What strange workmanship.

Thomas stood up and walked a few more feet down the tunnel. He didn't get far. Without warning, the stone below his feet fell away, dropping him thirty feet into a pool of water. Plummeting to the bottom, he pushed off the slimy floor with his feet and propelled himself back toward the surface.

Gasping for air, he shook his head to clear the water from his eyes. He was doing quite well, he thought sarcastically. Of the two traps he had discovered so far, he had fallen into both quite easily, and this one literally. Thomas swam over to the wall, which was covered by a slimy moss.

At least with this trap Thomas would have an easier time getting out. Pushing in on the indentation, his quarterstaff snapped into two. Thomas drove one blade into the wall just above where the water lapped against the stone, glad to see the ease with which the steel bit into it. He drove the other blade into the wall and then began the laborious process of pulling himself out of the water and up the wall.

Thomas stopped in mid-motion, a shiver of fear coursing through his body. What was that? Something had brushed against his legs. Something rough and scaly. Not wanting to find out what it was, Thomas hurriedly made his way up the wall. His feet were almost out of the water when something tightened around them and then jerked him downwards. His hands slipped off the spears, and he was pulled beneath the surface to the bottom of the pool.

Thomas struggled to get his head out of the water, but couldn't. The scaly skin was wrapped tightly around his feet, then his ankles, and was now moving quickly up his body. The darkness was complete underwater. Thomas could only make out the faintest of outlines of what had attacked him. As the scales tightened around his body, though, he didn't have to see the creature to know what he was up against.

A sea serpent! Why should he be surprised? Snakes seemed to be the preferred creature of the labyrinth. The scales continued to tighten around Thomas' body, forcing the breath from his lungs. He struggled against its grip, trying desperately to free his legs. Spots appeared before his eyes. He needed to breathe.

Confident in its victory, the snake coiled its scales around his chest then brought its head around toward Thomas' face. Even in the underwater gloom he saw the rows of sharp teeth bearing down on him. A very hungry snake. Normally they waited until their prey had suffocated before feasting, but not this one. Thomas had to do something — quickly! The spots appeared more and more frequently, clouding his vision. Time was running out, and with it his life.

As the snake's head surged forward, Thomas caught it in his hands, forcing the jaws apart. His strength was rapidly failing as darkness settled around the edges of his vision. He had been underwater too long. The strong coils of the snake were squeezing the life from him. He would not be able to hold back the fangs much longer.

Marshaling his will, Thomas opened himself to the Talent, taking in as much as he could. At the moment he could care less if Chertney discovered his skill. In a matter of seconds he would be dead anyway. Controlling the power within him, a sharp bolt of energy flashed out of Thomas' hand, striking the snake full in the face and killing it instantly.

Thomas would have breathed a sigh of relief if he could

have. But his lungs still begged for air and the coils of the snake remained wrapped around Thomas. The dead weight of the creature pulled him to the bottom of the pool. He struggled frantically to get free.

The darkness was almost upon him now, a vast, welcoming darkness, where he could forget his worries and just sleep. It seemed so inviting, so peaceful. No!

He retreated from the edge of the darkness waiting to engulf him. He needed air desperately. His lungs felt like they were about to explode. Struggling feverishly, Thomas unwrapped the heavy coils from his body, then pushed off of the bottom of the pool once more. As his head broke the surface of the water, he hungrily gasped for air.

Thomas didn't waste any time getting his breath back. Still gulping down air, he lunged for one of the blades still caught in the wall, thankful to take hold of it on his first attempt. He then began to pull himself up again, not wanting to be near the pool of water a second longer than necessary. He had no desire to find out if more than one sea snake lived beneath the Labyrinth. No desire at all.

Several minutes later he pulled himself over the edge of the hole and onto the floor of the passageway. He lay there for several minutes sucking in air, fully expecting the Makreen to appear at any second and not really caring. Once he breathed easier, he pushed himself to his feet and walked unsteadily but warily down the hallway, wanting to get off the large stone slabs as quickly as possible.

When he felt the surface of the passageway change beneath his feet from the stone slabs to roughly cut stone he finally breathed a sigh of relief and took a moment to gain his bearings. Two traps down. How many more remained, he didn't know.

42

NEW DANGER

Thomas had made his way through more than half of the Labyrinth now, and the Makreen had not yet reappeared. Though he had defeated two of the Labyrinth's traps, he much preferred fighting the Makreen, even with the beast's penchant for surprise. At least then he knew what he faced. Each trap offered a new danger, and he worried that if he didn't exit the Labyrinth soon, one trap eventually would get the better of him.

Though the blood had stopped flowing from the wound on his head, the slash on his ribs continued to bleed, and he could feel his strength slipping away with each step. Thomas pushed away the cobwebs that formed in his mind. He couldn't allow his exhaustion to take hold. Otherwise, he'd make a mistake. And in the Labyrinth, his first mistake would be his last.

The tunnel had not changed since he had escaped from the sea serpent. At least he didn't have to worry about that. Still, for the last few minutes he had heard a strange rustling noise coming from behind him. Faint at first, it had grown in intensity. He continued to follow the map in his head, at the same time trying to determine the cause of the noise. As the minutes slipped away, the skittering sound behind him grew louder.

Stopping for a moment, Thomas extended his senses back along the way he had come. He immediately dashed off down the tunnel, pumping his legs as fast as he could. He could understand now why the Makreen had not bothered to come after him. There was no need.

Thomas ran down the tunnels, the map still in his mind, almost falling as he sped around several sharp corners. The noise behind him increased. He wasn't going to make it. Looking back as he turned another corner, a giant rat — about three feet in length — bounded around the corner after him, chittering in anticipation, its sharp teeth exposed. Behind the first rat came the rest of the pack, scrambling over one another, their desire for food driving them on.

Another branch appeared before Thomas as the lead rat nipped at his heels. Thomas stopped suddenly, swinging the quarterstaff behind him and gutting the rodent with the blade. He immediately kicked the body off the weapon and ran around the corner. He heard the pack stop for a moment, followed by the frantic sounds of the scramble for food. Then the rats continued the chase, devouring the wounded animal in seconds.

Thomas ran as fast as he could down the tunnel, the maneuver having bought him a little extra time. But not enough. The pack was gaining on him, the skittering of the hundreds of clawed feet scratching against the stone setting his teeth on edge. Panting heavily, the wound in his side continued to bleed and ached with every pounding step.

Thomas stopped again, swinging his quarterstaff in front of him with renewed energy borne of desperation. The sharp steel blades tore into the furry bodies. Not waiting to see how many he had killed, Thomas ran off again, hoping he had gained more time.

The bulk of the rats milled around the carcasses, hungrily consuming them. Yet it took less than a minute before the pack stripping the bodies to the bone. The rats continued the chase. His fear driving him forward, Thomas tried to think of a way to escape. Nothing came to mind. He was still too far away from the exit. All he could do was try to slow the pack down and hope an opportunity presented itself. He knew it wasn't much of a plan. Soon his weariness would get the better of him. Then the rats would have him.

Lost in his thoughts, Thomas stumbled and almost fell, a rat having snapped at his heel. Thomas stabbed the creature in the back, then swung the quarterstaff around to meet the charge of two more rats. This time, though he killed the two rats, his movements were awkward. The first rat was still lodged onto the other blade, weighing him down.

Several more rats charged forward. Thomas frantically spun the quarterstaff above his head in a whipping motion. The dead rat's body flew off the staff behind him and landed on the floor. In an instant the walls slammed together, crushing the body into something unrecognizable, then just as fast sliding back into place.

Thomas couldn't believe it. Swinging the quarterstaff in front of him, he plowed through the rats, yet even more came forward. Though he might decimate the pack, in the end the rats would win. Their numbers were too great, and with the newly discovered trap behind him, he had nowhere to go. Then again, perhaps the trap would work to his advantage this time.

As a rat leapt through the air for his throat, Thomas caught it on his blade, but instead of throwing it to the pack he turned and ran down the hallway. Just before he reached the crushed carcass, he threw the rat off his spear. The body landed beside what had once been the other rat. The walls slammed together, crushing the rat, then began moving back to their original positions. This time, though, with the walls still in motion, in a burst of speed fueled by fear, Thomas bolted down the tunnel, diving through to the other side just before the walls crashed together again. The rats that chased after him weren't so lucky.

Thomas sat there on the floor for a brief moment catching his breath. The mass of rats stopped, unwilling to chance the walls, more than satisfied to gorge themselves on the carcasses left for them by Thomas. Thankfully he had been right. The walls had to fully return to their original position before coming together again. Even so, he had barely made it through. If he had been wearing boots, he probably would have lost a foot.

Shivering at such a thought, Thomas pushed himself back up. Not wanting to waste more time, Thomas trotted down the tunnel. The Labyrinth was almost at an end, and he knew the Makreen waited for him. Thomas smiled in anticipation. He didn't want to disappoint his adversary.

43

MURMURS

Kaylie wrung her hands in worry as the minutes slipped by, her concern for Thomas increasing. Sarelle leaned past Gregory from time to time, trying to engage her in conversation in an attempt to distract her, but to no avail. The murmurs within the crowd grew more intense, the wagers increasing. The entire spectacle sickened her.

She took some solace that as the minutes dragged by, Rodric seemed to worry more, cringing every time Lord Chertney leaned forward to whisper angrily in his ear.

Perhaps Thomas could survive, she thought. Fearhounds and Ogren didn't seem to bother him. So why couldn't he escape the Makreen?

A wish in vain, maybe, but it was the only thing she could hold onto as her fears played through her mind.

44

ALMOST AT AN END

Thomas crept silently down the corridor, his eyes sweeping from side to side. The exit to the maze was just ahead at the end of the tunnel. He held his quarterstaff at the ready, expecting an attack at any time. His anticipation increased as he drew closer to the portal. According to the map, a large, circular room awaited him, and through that was the pit — and Thomas' freedom.

As he came to the entrance, Thomas let go of the Talent. He knew which way to go now, and his constant use of the power was draining what little energy he had left. Besides, he didn't want to take any chances with Chertney so close.

Carefully stepping through the threshold, Thomas swept his eyes over the room. It resembled an oversized banquet hall and was probably large enough to seat five hundred or more. On the far side light cut into the darkness through a doorway, shining brightly in an otherwise nebulous environment. Thomas smiled. The pit, and freedom. Still, it couldn't be this easy. His suspicions were confirmed quickly.

"You've done well."

The raspy, guttural voice broke the silence of the hall.

Thomas' eyes followed the sound, picking out the shadowy creature standing calmly in the center of the room. The beast had acquired another quarterstaff, leaning his weight on it. Though its huge body was shrouded in darkness, its red eyes burned brightly.

"None have ever made it to my sanctuary." Thomas struggled to decipher some of the words, as the Makreen had difficulty pronouncing certain sounds because of the forked tongue that slithered from its mouth. "Normally I like to kill my prey at the beginning of the maze, as you might have guessed, if only so I don't have to wait for my traps to claim them."

The Makreen shifted his weight, standing up straight and holding his quarterstaff with two hands.

"But you, green eyes, you are different. I wondered if you would make it this far."

"And I have," responded Thomas.

"You have," said the Makreen. "Thank you for the entertainment, but now it must come to an end. The Labyrinth is my domain, and only one can rule here. Only I can rule here!"

The Makreen shouted the words to emphasize his point.

"Then let us begin," said Thomas calmly.

He had been through more than he thought possible in the last two days. He wanted it to end, and the only way to ensure that was to make his way out into the pit. But he would have to get there first. The sooner he started, the sooner he would be done — one way or the other.

The Makreen nodded. In a rush, the Makreen charged forward, one tip of the quarterstaff held out like a spear.

Though Thomas was tired, the Makreen's attempt to take him by surprise by the sudden burst of motion failed. Thomas easily stepped aside, avoiding the charge. The two combatants began circling one another, twirling their quarterstaffs in front of them, ready for one or the other to make the next move.

The Makreen obviously had the advantage of size and

strength on his side, the beast towering above him, but Thomas was faster. Therefore he chose to wait and study the Makreen's pattern of attack before making his move. After coming so far, now was not the time to make a foolish mistake.

Impatient for the kill, the Makreen ran forward again, lunging twice then slashing at his face. Thomas deflected the first two blows and ducked under the third. The Makreen stepped back, smiling. He was enjoying the contest and was certain of his victory, sensing his opponent's fatigue.

They circled each other once again. This time the Makreen didn't wait as long to attack. Lunging forward with the quarterstaff, the beast slashed at Thomas, aiming for his legs. When Thomas blocked the blow, the beast immediately brought the quarterstaff up and cut at Thomas' neck.

Thomas raised his staff just in time, stopping the blow from connecting, the Makreen's blade barely missing its intended target. Thomas pushed the Makreen back, finding a renewed energy within himself, then slashed with his own quarterstaff, forcing the Makreen to break off.

The contest continued in much the same way for the next few minutes. The Makreen circled Thomas, waiting for an opening to attack. Each time the creature charged forward, Thomas defended himself. Yet each time the Makreen maintained his attack for just a little bit longer.

Thomas realized what the Makreen was doing. The beast had noticed that the cut on Thomas' side had reopened, and as a result, it was only a matter time before his weakness proved fatal. Until then, the Makreen was simply playing with him, waiting until Thomas' reactions slowed. He had to change tactics. Otherwise, Thomas would die just a few feet from his goal.

As the Makreen lunged forward once again, instead of catching the blade on his own, Thomas ducked beneath the slash and swung low with his own blade. Carried forward by his momentum, the Makreen left himself exposed, and Thomas sliced him across the back of his leg. The Makreen leapt away, howling in anger and pain. Rather than wait for the next attack, Thomas became the aggressor, refusing to give the Makreen time to recover.

Continuing his attack, Thomas maneuvered the beast toward the opening of light. Try as he might, the Makreen could not disengage himself from the flurry of lunges, slashes and chops, the injury to the back of his leg limiting his mobility. All the Makreen could do now was focus on defending himself. Thomas ignored his tired muscles as he continued his assault. His quarterstaff was a blur of motion, and the arrogance and hunger in the eyes of the Makreen slowly changed to desperation.

Only wanting to break away, the Makreen jumped backwards, trying to gain some breathing room. But his injured leg failed him, and rather than stepping out of the way, he stumbled, giving Thomas another opportunity. Thomas' slash took the Makreen across the back of the other leg.

The Makreen howled again, this time in pain and fear. This tiny man was winning. The Makreen tried to break away again, hoping to slip off into the darkness, but Thomas wouldn't allow it. The beast only had two options: deal with Thomas or back away through the entrance to the pit.

Not really having much of a choice, the Makreen stepped through the entrance with Thomas right behind him, slashing and lunging with his quarterstaff, seeking another exposed part of the Makreen's body. All thought had left Thomas' mind. All he had now was motion, constant motion. The quarterstaff had become a part of him. He didn't even notice when the darkness gave way to light.

45

FAINT HOPE

As each minute passed Kaylie's hope that Thomas was still alive increased just a bit more. He had been in the Labyrinth for more than an hour, closer to two in fact. Many of the lords and ladies filling the gallery looked down at the white sand with disgust. They had bet on a quick end and lost their money as a result. Rodric's growing concern was evident, even though Loris said there was nothing to fear. If the boy had fallen victim to one of the traps, which probably had happened, it would take the Makreen longer than usual to bring his body out into the pit.

A new murmur had begun to run through the crowd, as many discussed the boy's chances of survival. None had ever stayed in the Labyrinth for so long, or so the stories said. There were others in the crowd who scoffed at such a possibility, arguing that the Makreen was probably just playing with the body before dragging it out.

Kaylie tried to ignore the chatter. It was because of her that Thomas was down there to begin with. Could he really still be alive? She hoped so with all her heart.

A sudden uproar in the gallery forced Kaylie's eyes to the

white sand of the pit. She gasped in shock at the scene unfolding before her. The Makreen had just backed out of the Labyrinth, and right behind him came Thomas, his entire body a whirlwind of motion as he drove the beast backwards. Thomas was covered in blood, yet his green eyes blazed fiercely. Kaylie wanted to cry with joy. In her heart, she knew what the outcome would be.

46

FREEDOM

Thomas didn't hear the startled gasps or notice the shocked expressions of the onlookers as he stepped out into the light. He knew he had made it to the pit because he could feel the grainy particles of white sand slip through his toes. He remained focused completely on his task, his mind free of everything but one desire — to kill the Makreen.

Despite his quickly tiring body and the wound in his side screaming for him to stop, Thomas followed after the beast, his quarterstaff coming ever closer to its primary goal. It was only a matter of time before his opportunity would come. He had to be ready.

The crowd gasped anew when the Makreen dropped to one knee, one injured leg having finally given out. Seeing the opening he had worked so hard for, Thomas raised his quarterstaff above his head and brought it down toward the skull of the Makreen. The beast grasped its quarterstaff with both hands and raised it above his head to defend against the blow.

Expecting such a tactic, Thomas pressed on the slight indentation in the haft of the quarterstaff. While still bringing one blade down with his right hand, he pulled free the other half, slashing toward the Makreen's throat. The Makreen never saw it coming. The blade cut halfway into its neck, its life gushing from the wound and staining the white sand red.

He should have felt jubilation, but at the moment he was hollow on the inside. Thomas stepped back as the Makreen collapsed onto its side, its eyes blank and staring. It was over. Unexpectedly, pride surged within him. He had just shoved another thorn into Rodric's foot, and this one quite deeply.

Finally he looked up into the gallery, which had gone deathly quiet. He saw all the stunned faces, even Kaylie's, as no one had expected such an end. Breathing heavily, Thomas threw the other half of the quarterstaff's blade into the sand. He stood there proudly, enjoying the look of confusion on Rodric's face. He could read the High King's thoughts quite clearly. *This wasn't supposed to happen*, he could see running behind those beady eyes. *This wasn't supposed to happen!* Even Chertney was at a loss as to what to do. No one wanted to break the silence. Finally, someone did.

"The boy has made it through the Labyrinth and killed the Makreen," said Gregory as he rose from his seat. "He has passed the Trial."

"He has passed the Trial," seconded Sarelle, as did several other lords and ladies still dumbfounded by what had occurred. The Makreen had never before been defeated. How could this boy have won?

"According to the law, then, he is innocent," said Gregory. "He is free."

Rodric turned his eyes to the King of Fal Carrach, still not sure what had gone wrong. He looked for some way to turn this situation around, but he couldn't. He had been bested by this boy, just like his son.

"He is free," whispered Rodric, the words a struggle for him to get out.

Gregory nodded in satisfaction and Kaylie sighed with

relief. She looked down at Thomas, trying to apologize with her eyes, but he refused to acknowledge her. Instead, he scanned the crowd with a defiant glare. His eyes came to rest on Rodric, who found the gaze uncomfortable, but to look away now would be a sign of weakness.

Pleased to see Rodric's sullen expression, Thomas was distracted for a moment by a young girl with long blonde hair sitting next to him. She was quite beautiful, and judging by her pursed lips and crossed arms, she weighed him. It made him extremely uncomfortable. He could tell right away that she was probably just as dangerous as the Makreen, if not more so.

Finally he glanced at Kaylie. Her eyes begged his forgiveness. He quickly looked away. The wound of her betrayal was still fresh, and he was not yet ready to forgive, if he ever would be. As he stood there, his pose one of defiance and pride, something tickled the back of his mind.

He suddenly felt with a great deal of certainty that he had foreseen the whole moment — of Kaylie looking down at him as he was covered in blood, victorious like the gladiators of old in the white sand of the pit. The scene continued to play along the edges of his memory, but he couldn't place it. No matter. He had accomplished his goal. He was free.

THE END

Keep reading for the first four chapters of Book 5, *The Lord of the Highlands*.

BONUS MATERIAL

If you really enjoyed this story, I need you to do me a HUGE favor – please follow me on Amazon and BookBub.

And if you have a few minutes, consider writing a review.

Keep reading for the first four chapters of Book 5 of *The Sylvan Chronicles, The Lord of the Highlands.*

PETER WACHT

THE LORD OF THE HIGHLANDS

THE SYLVAN CHRONICLES

5

ISBN: 978-1-950236-08-4

eBook ISBN: 978-1-950236-09-1

Library of Congress Control Number: 2020900164

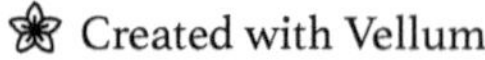 Created with Vellum

1. SOON TO HUNT

The raptor flew low over the trees, its long tail feathers barely missing the topmost branches. The bird of prey welcomed the rush of speed as its powerful wings brought it closer to the monstrous monolith that dominated the lush, green valley. The massive stone reared up before the magnificent bird. Tilting its wings, the raptor drifted to the left, catching an upward draft so that it could negotiate its way to the top.

As it circled the black, sheer stone, the raptor gradually gained altitude. The orange feathers lining its back glinted brightly as they caught the sun's rays, in contrast to the black and brown feathers that absorbed the light's energy. The heat from the sun energized the bird, building on the urgency it already felt. The raptor had seen much on its long journey through Fal Carrach, the kingdom that sat below the Highlands, as it watched from high above the earth.

Raptors were solitary creatures, defending a specific territory. That territory often stretched for dozens of leagues in every direction, limiting the contact between these ferocious birds of prey. A meeting of raptors was even rarer because they were so few in number. Nobles and other fortune seekers had hunted them almost to extinction during the last hundred years, hoping to turn a profit with the carcass of these legendary animals.

Strangely, since entering the Highlands from the south and finally reaching the Valley of the Crag, it had met three raptors. Yet, it was something else that made the creature wonder if the world was changing.

Reaching the top of the promontory, the raptor looked down on what had once been the mighty fortress of a mighty people. Selecting the highest vantage point, the bird settled onto the crumbling stone of one of the collapsed towers of the keep, its razor-sharp claws holding it steady as the strong winds of the Highlands tried to unseat it.

Meeting three of its kind in so short a span was unique, but that in itself wasn't enough to make the raptor look at the world differently. No, it was what the bird had observed in the south, something it had never expected to see. It was still early, perhaps too early to tell for sure if the sense of urgency the raptor felt building within it was justified. The great bird sensed a shift in nature itself, and that shift was beginning here – at the Crag.

Less than a decade before, the Crag had served as the capital of the Highlands -- and home to the Marchers. Reputedly the best fighters in all the Kingdoms, as with any warrior, even the Marchers had a weakness. The Highlands was a rugged and dangerous land, and the same could be said of the Marchers, but, like the raptors, they were few in number.

When the betrayal occurred almost ten years before, though the Marchers fought valiantly, they could not prevent the inevitable. A once mighty fortress fell, and a once mighty people were defeated. Since that time, the plateau atop the monolith had lain abandoned. Moss had sprouted between the stones and the forest began its quest to reclaim its stolen territory.

The raptor shifted its right claw, adjusting for the wind. That tiny movement knocked away a small piece of moss, revealing the black stone beneath. Here, atop the Crag, the raptor felt the shift in nature even more, conscious of its growing strength and purpose. It sensed a new beginning. Hot blood was beginning to flow once more in the Highlands, beginning to stir, perhaps even boil, but only time would tell.

For it was still early. But it was still a beginning. The Highlands was again showing signs of life after ten years of treachery and oppression. And much like nature itself, the people of the Highlands were an unforgiving lot. For centuries, it had been said that like a raptor, to risk the wrath of a Marcher was to risk death – or worse.

As the raptor studied the harsh landscape of the Highlands, the sun began its slow descent in the west. Soon it would hunt, taking advantage of the dim light for an easy meal, for no creature could withstand the fury of a raptor's attack as the large bird hurtled down from the sky with breathtaking speed, its powerful wings drawn in, its sharp claws extended for its prey, the bird no more than a grey shadow in the sky. Much like the attack of a Marcher.

2. THE FEAST

"You still don't know if he has been freed?" Gregory whispered, not wanting Kaylie to overhear.

"No, milord," answered Kael, the Swordmaster bending down to keep his words discreet. "I haven't been able to find out a thing. None of the soldiers or servants are talking."

In any palace, the servants usually knew more of what was going on than anyone else. Keeping a secret in such a place was almost impossible. Yet this one had been kept, acknowledged Kael, and that's what worried him.

"It bothers me, milord."

"Me as well," said Gregory, who gave Sarelle a meaningful look.

The Queen of Benewyn sat next to Gregory at the head table in the main dining hall of the Palace, and on his other side sat Kaylie. They looked out on the dozens of tables below them filled with revelers. The Eastern Festival was coming to a close with a banquet to celebrate the contests won, the goods sold and the agreements made for the coming year.

"I think Rodric is up to something," said Sarelle.

She wore a dark green dress that set off her auburn hair

perfectly. When Gregory had come to escort her to the banquet, upon seeing her he had become distinctly uncomfortable, just as Sarelle had desired. Yet her thoughts turned from romantic conquests to other things when Kael appeared. His report worried her as well. Something stirred in the Palace, and it wasn't for the good.

"I agree," said Gregory. "We should have had word of the boy's leaving by now."

"Agreed, milord." Kael, too, had gotten a bad feeling about this evening. "I've already alerted the men. We're packed and ready to go whenever you give the command."

Kael turned to Sarelle. "I've instructed Captain Fornier to do the same, Queen Sarelle. I hope that was not presumptuous of me."

"No, not at all," she replied, thankful that he had thought to prepare the captain of her guard. "I hope the good captain did not put up much of a fuss."

"He didn't, Queen Sarelle. He sensed it too and had already begun his own preparations. I've asked him to wait at the stables just in case the need arises. The men of Fal Carrach wait nearby."

Gregory smiled briefly. Leave it to Kael to think of everything. There had been no outward signs of trouble, yet little things had pricked at Gregory's sense of danger since the Trial. A few extra guards here, a few extra guards there. Restrictions on leaving the Palace. Subdued and quiet servants.

"Thank you, Kael. You've done well, as always."

"I simply do as you command, milord."

Kael stepped down from the dais and made his way out of the hall, wanting to sniff around for more clues. Gregory watched him go, thankful once again that Kael Bellilil had accepted his offer of employment so many years before.

"A good man there," said Sarelle.

"The best," answered Gregory.

He glanced to his right, checking on his daughter. It didn't appear as if she had heard anything. Good. He didn't want her to start worrying again.

Kaylie took no notice of the brief conversation held between her father, Sarelle and Kael. Her thoughts were elsewhere. When Thomas defeated the Makreen, a huge weight had been lifted from her chest. She hoped that he was back in the forest by now, and as far away from Tinnakilly as possible. Her eyes wandered over the hall several times, yet always came back to the young woman sitting a few seats to the right of the High King.

Corelia. She had shown far too much interest in Thomas after his victory. Far too much. Kaylie eyed the Princess of Armagh with suspicion. Corelia did nothing without good reason. As her eyes drifted down the head table, she locked gazes with Ragin for a brief moment, who gave her a leer that set her face afire. She tore her eyes away from him. Ragin had absolutely no shame. She was a fool for even being attracted to him at one time.

She was about to ask her father what he had been saying to Kael when she realized that conversation had died down within hall, the loud rumble of many voices talking and laughing replaced by almost total silence. Looking toward the front of the hall, she gasped in shock. Her father jumped up from his chair, knocking it backward in his haste, his face red with anger.

"What is the meaning of this, Rodric?" he demanded. "The boy passed the Trial. He was to be set free!"

Thomas stood in the doorway, his legs and wrists chained. Two very large Dunmoorian soldiers dragged him into the banquet hall and past the startled revelers until he stood in front of the head table. Thomas appeared tired, yet defiant. His body was covered in bruises and dried blood, and no one had tended to his two wounds — the one on his forehead, the other on his side.

"True, Gregory," said Rodric, sitting comfortably in his chair as if nothing was amiss. "But it was not to be so. It seems the boy cannot suppress his true nature. Soon after he defeated the Makreen, we attempted to clean his wounds before letting him go. Throwing him out through the gates without any medical attention would have been inhumane."

The irony of what the High King had just said was not lost on those in the hall.

"Yet he would not allow us to help. The boy stabbed one physick with his own scalpel, nearly killing him. And he injured several of my men when they tried to bring him under control."

"And where is this physick?" asked Gregory. "And your injured men?"

Rodric was lying through his teeth, but Gregory could do nothing about it. His worst fear was becoming a reality and explained the tense atmosphere of the Palace. Rodric never had any intention of letting the boy go. That realization set his mind wondering once again as to why this boy was so important to him.

He remained standing, flexing his fists in an effort to control his temper. Rodric was flouting the laws of the Kingdoms with this charade, yet no one was in a position to stop him. This was not a good sign at all. He glanced quickly to the back of the hall and saw Kael standing by the door. The Highlander nodded. At least they were prepared. Now the question was, what could he do about this, if anything?

"In the infirmary, I'm afraid. Their severe injuries prevent them from being here."

Rodric had expected such a question from Gregory, knowing he would not be satisfied with his explanation. In fact, he had created his own casualties to complete the scheme if needed.

"It was truly an unfortunate episode, yet if you need proof, my son Ragin was there, and I'm sure he'd be willing to fill in all the details."

All eyes in the banquet hall turned to Ragin, who looked back rather smugly. He studied Thomas for a moment, pleased by his condition, before slowly rising from his chair.

3. ON THE TRAIL

"Two or three days old," said Catal Huyuk, rising from where he crouched in the grass.

"As I thought," grunted Rynlin, not really paying attention.

Rynlin had met Beluil in the clearing at the western edge of Oakwood Forest in the late morning. Luckily, Catal Huyuk was actually on the way to the Isle of Mist when he answered Rynlin's call for help, sensing his need through his necklace. Beluil waited impatiently at one side of the clearing, eager to continue the hunt.

"Thomas put up quite a fight," said the dangerous-looking man, the blades of his many weapons gleaming in the sun. As he walked around the glade, he replayed the skirmish through his mind. "He was heavily outnumbered, but killed four or five, maybe more. He must have fought like a demon." Pride was clear in his voice.

Rynlin continued to stare at a particular spot in the grass, his anger raging within him. As soon as he arrived in the clearing, he had searched the surrounding area thoroughly, looking for some clue as to what had happened. Eventually, he came back to the blanket and basket of food — and the wine bottle.

One sniff told him everything he needed to know. Once again someone had taken his grandson. His grandson! His only grandson!

"Let's get going," Rynlin said, coming out of his trance. "The Eastern Festival is coming to a close. There's only one place he could have been taken."

Catal Huyuk nodded, following after Rynlin and Beluil as they walked out onto the grasslands. Thomas was Rynlin's grandson, but for Catal Huyuk he was something more — hope for the future, a bright light to follow in the coming darkness. Whoever had taken Thomas had made a grave mistake.

4. CHANGING WINDS

"Lords and ladies, it is ... it is true."

Ragin's voice wavered. Gregory's open disbelief unnerved him a bit. Ragin scanned the back of the banquet hall, the dozens of Armaghian soldiers lining the walls renewing his confidence.

"The physick attempted to examine his wounds. We expected him to be tired, to be grateful for the attention, but no."

Ragin appeared saddened by what he was about to relate. "He grabbed a scalpel from the physick's bag and stabbed the good man in the gut. He then went after me and my men, several of whom were injured while subduing him. After a great deal of struggle, we finally stopped him from injuring anyone else. As the Prince of Armagh, I swear it as the truth."

Ragin immediately dropped back into his seat at a barely noticeable motion from his father. He had wanted to say more, perhaps embellish his role in the charade, but his father had told him exactly what to say — and to say only that. By the feverish look in his father's eyes, now was not the time to cross him.

Kaylie looked from her father to Rodric. The two were locked in a battle of wills. For the first time she saw a murderous glare on her father's face and knew for a fact that if Rodric stood any closer, the High King would be dead. Her anger matched her father's, that and her disbelief.

Ragin swore as Prince of Armagh! The thought was ludicrous. Everyone knew him to be a liar, yet no one would challenge him. Not here anyway. Kaylie could see that her father had already considered such an action, but wisely chose not to. When Thomas entered the chamber, the soldiers of Dunmoor and Armagh silently had taken up positions along the back wall.

There was nothing she or her father could do. Gregory cursed in frustration, knowing full well that even though his men could defeat the soldiers of any other Kingdom, they were outnumbered here at the Palace. Even with the addition of Sarelle's troops, the skirmish would be a short one.

Gregory suddenly realized what he was considering. An uprising against the High King? In the middle of Dunmoor? Some might call it treason, others a necessity. Times had changed drastically in just a few days, and for the worse. Rodric was pushing against the fragile balance of power within the Kingdoms. If he continued, that balance would disintegrate.

"Obviously you have taken every precaution, Rodric. You have won this time, but this is only the first battle." Gregory sat back down in his chair, gripping the ornately carved wooden arms tightly.

The audience watched the entire episode in rapt attention, sensing that a change of some sort was taking place. What effect it would have was still in question, yet all knew it revolved around the boy standing before the head table — the boy in chains, his body covered in blood, bruises and cuts; the boy who had defeated the Makreen; the boy who should be free. Anyone with the tiniest bit of political sense knew that Rodric had orchestrated a sham, but like Gregory, they too saw the Armaghian and Dunmoorian soldiers standing behind them.

"Then justice will finally be done," said Rodric, motioning to a guard standing by the door, who immediately ran out into the hallway shouting orders.

Kaylie stared at Thomas with tears in her eyes. He was going to die, and it was all her fault. She could hear her father cursing softly next to her, Sarelle's hand covering his own to offer comfort, his voice rife with frustration at not being able to help the boy standing before them. The words tyranny, murder and false accusation mixed with greed and power as Gregory spouted an invective-filled tirade. She glanced quickly at Rodric. Next to him Ragin smiled with glee, clearly enjoying the spectacle unfolding before him.

Corelia, on the other hand, studied Thomas much like a predator before a kill. The look she gave him — calculating, shrewd, suggestive — made her skin crawl. There had to be something Kaylie could do. Anything. She leaned forward in her chair, her grief threatening to overwhelm her. It was hopeless. There was nothing for her to do but watch the one person who had treated her as a friend die because of her foolishness.

"We have a criminal before us," intoned Rodric, speaking as a judge would before an execution. "Justice will be done. Bring him here."

The two guards standing behind Thomas shoved him forward, knocking him to the ground because of the chains around his ankles.

"Perhaps the demonstration that follows will show that such crimes are not permitted in the Kingdoms, and that as High King, I will do whatever necessary to ensure my law is upheld."

Many of the lords and ladies turned shocked expressions to the High King, realizing the true meaning of his words. Rodric was going to punish the boy right here. More important, he had said *my law*. Not *the law*. Murmurs of discontent ran through the crowd, but quickly ceased when several Armaghian soldiers stepped forward. The winds of change blew strong and cold.

The soldier quickly returned, followed by a dozen more pushing a cart carrying a large piece of wood. It resembled something the hangman would use, in that the two large pieces of oak ran perpendicular to one another. At the end of the smaller piece another block of oak ran crosshairs to it. Attached to that piece were long black chains with manacles affixed to their ends.

The soldiers moved slowly toward the head table, grunting with effort as they approached. Everyone watched in horrified fascination as the soldiers set one end of the wood structure onto the bottom of the cart.

The two soldiers guarding Thomas then removed the manacles from his wrists and ankles, revealing the bloody skin rubbed raw by the steel, and placed the other manacles around his wrists. The soldiers then used rope tied to the top of the piece of wood to pull the structure upright, dragging Thomas backward until he was hoisted into the air. They then placed several steel pins at the foot of the wood block to keep it in position.

To Kaylie, it seemed as if Thomas had been placed on the gallows. The chains spread Thomas' arms wide, tearing open the wound in his side once more. A slow trickle of blood began to run down his leg, dripping from his foot onto the cart floorboards. Kaylie wanted to avert her eyes, as many of the ladies in the banquet hall had already done, unable to bear the condition Thomas was in. Instead, she forced herself to look at him.

As her eyes ran over his body, she saw the many scars

running across his back and chest, the very sight of them making her sick to her stomach. Still, she refused to look away. During the past two days Thomas had demonstrated remarkable courage. She would try to do the same, little good that it would do.

"I see you are not a stranger to the whip," said Rodric. "Good. Then you are familiar with what is to happen next. I will save you from the pain if you will admit your guilt. Will you, boy? Will you admit your guilt?"

Rodric did not wait for a response, not really expecting, or even wanting, one. This lesson was only in part for Thomas. He motioned to a soldier standing by the hangman's block who held a barbed whip in his hand. He stepped behind Thomas, flicking the long, black leather behind his back before swinging forward violently. The whip dug deeply into Thomas' flesh, the sharp crack echoing in the silent chamber. The soldier drew the whip back again, and again, until each sharp crack drifted into the one preceding it.

Gregory felt sick to his stomach. Everyone in the hall knew what Rodric had planned for Thomas, yet still he had to go through with this act. This wasn't justice. This was revenge. This was a statement. And for what? Gregory promised himself that he would find out, and that he would pay back Rodric many times over for the pain he caused this innocent boy. Gregory's futility ate into his heart, filling it with despair. The boy had saved his life, and his daughter's life twice, and he could not return the favor.

Thomas kept his head lowered as the whip bit sharply into his flesh. He was beyond pain now. His waning energy decreased with each strike of the barbed leather. He wanted only to escape the pain now, having lost the desire to fight. He had driven his body too far. Now he just wanted to rest, to let go. The struggle had become too much to bear.

I hope you enjoyed the first four chapters. To keep reading *The Lord of the Highlands*, Book 5 of *The Sylvan Chronicles*, order your copy today from www.PeterWachtBooks.com or from Amazon.

This short story is a prelude to the events in my series *The Tales of Caledonia* and is free to readers who receive my newsletter.

Join Peter's newsletter and get your FREE short story at www.PeterWachtBooks.com.